THE AMAZING BULK

A NOVEL BY
ATOM MUDMAN BEZECNY

BASED ON THE FILM CREATED BY
LEWIS SCHOENBRUN, KEITH SCHAFFNER, AND JEREMIAH CAMPBELL

Encyclopocalypse Publications
www.encyclopocalypse.com

First Edition, 2025
ISBN: 978-1-966037-36-1

Original artwork from the TomCat Films DVD release used by permission.
Layout and design by Sean Duregger
Interior formatting by Sean Duregger
Edited by Mike Watt

THE AMAZING BULK

0.

It was, to coin a phrase, a dark and stormy night.

The whole city was swept with thick torrents of rain, and the clouds above masked the stars and moon; even the streetlights, which were much closer to the Earth, strained to spread light through the downpour. The wind turned the raindrops into blistering ice-cold spears, and there was no escape from their stabbing force. It was as miserable as it could get.

For Minnie Modino, it was worse than miserable. She should've checked the forecast for the evening. Now she was stuck running through the rain in—what were these, five inch heels?

Five inch heels and *fishnets*. God, her legs were *drenched*. Her top was soaked through. She was a mess. A cold, shivering, out-of-breath mess.

It had been a long night. But then, for a hooker, every night was a long one.

Minnie was a hooker—and she was a self-described hooker. She realized it wasn't a pleasant appellation for a lot of people, but it was a frank one. The better term, supposedly, was "sex worker," but in her mind that was an umbrella term, separate from the specifics of her job. Minnie had some pride in calling herself a hooker, because there was no ambiguity about how she made her living. She could just go up to people and say something like, "Hey, I'm a hooker," and chances were they'd know right away what she meant.

But she knew she was a rare type. She always had been…

Damn, she needed a cigarette. She knew it would be impossible in this rain, but she took out her matches anyway. She'd found a spot in an alley under the stone lip of a building where it was sort of dry.

Only two matches left. She struck one and the head broke off. "Shit," she said. She tried to strike the second, but the wind was too strong. "Shit!"

If only she didn't enjoy the wood-smoked taste of match-lit cigarettes, and invested in a lighter instead.

Just then, a flame snapped into view before her eyes. That flame came from a Zippo, which in turn came from the hand of a leering man in a dark coat.

"Shit," Minnie whispered.

"Need a light?" the man cackled. His other hand was now visible, and in it was some sort of handgun.

"How 'bout you suck on this?"

He must've deduced her line of work.

Before she knew it, he had crammed the snout of the gun in her mouth. At once, terror flooded her body. She felt her eyes go wide as she stared in horror at her attacker.

"Yeah…I figured you'd done that before."

With his finger on the trigger he rifled through her pockets. With one hand he took out the bag of condoms she'd been carrying.

"I appreciate your sense of responsibility, darlin', but these ain't gonna protect you now."

He scattered the plastic-wrapped rubbers on the ground.

Then he went for the other pocket. He pulled out her take for the night—nearly a grand in cash.

"Now that's more like it!"

He crammed the money in his pocket. "These are going straight into the Bank of My Blue Jeans," he chuckled.

He kept the gun in her mouth. Then, his eyes began to study her body. A horrible light came into those eyes.

"You make one move, I decorate the wall with your brains."

Minnie wasn't going anywhere, despite her wish to the contrary.

"Hey, don't worry. I used to be a pimp, you know. I know how to treat women…"

She wished she could speak so she could beg to be let go.

Just then, there was a rush of movement behind him—and with it, a horrible noise. It was deafening, like the roar of some terrible beast. The ex-pimp mugger flinched with terror—and in doing so, his trigger finger twitched. And just like that, Minnie was dead.

"Oh, fuck," the killer gasped. "Oh, no, no, I didn't want it to be murder…"

But he had other problems. *Big* problems. Once again, the bestial roar split the air—

And with a scream of pants-shitting terror, the mugger and killer met a horrible fate of his own.

The world didn't notice. It kept on turning.

It kept on turning until day bloomed over the city, and the rain which had helped ruin the night of an innocent woman was gone.

1.

Police tape surrounded the battered corpse of "Scully" Hayden, the mugger and former pimp. The body of his victim had already been taken away by the medical exam team. It was easy to determine that Hayden had been the one to kill the dead sex worker—he'd had the gun in his hand, and the bullets in the gun matched the one they found in Minnie Modino's head. As for who killed *him*, though—well, that was what Garton and Tuttle were trying to figure out.

Garton and Tuttle were the detectives assigned to the case. They were considered top of their field, the best in the city—they almost always got their man. Tuttle's hard, practiced face twitched slightly as she took notes in a small yellow pad, while bald-headed Garton was off in his own corner, hunching down to inspect the scene carefully.

Something stood out to Garton's eyes. He stroked his chin thoughtfully.

"Hey, Lisa, come over here."

Tuttle looked up from her pad and walked up to him.

"What's that?" she asked, pointing.

"That's what I was gonna ask you," Garton replied. "Looks like blood or something. I dunno."

"I never saw purple blood before."

But that's what it did look like. Blood, but purple.

Tuttle produced a small glass sample tube and a latex glove. Donning the latter, she knelt down and swept up some of the substance. It proved slightly gelatinous to the touch, like the borax putty that kids made for science projects. She corked the sample tube, wiped it clean, and put it in the evidence kit.

"This crime scene is turning out to be one big mystery," she said.

Garton snorted derisively. "No kidding. Did the examiners find anything else?"

"Just this."

From the same kit where she'd placed the blood sample, she pulled out a small leather wallet.

"It was in Hayden's coat. Definitely not his. Probably took it from some poor fool earlier tonight."

Garton popped it open.

"Henry Howard? Who the hell is this?"

Lisa shrugged. "Beats me. But I figure we'll find out soon enough."

Garton stared at the image of Henry Howard. There was something about that face he didn't like.

Maybe it was because it deepened the strange sense of dread he'd felt upon seeing how badly beaten the mugger was. Only a monster could do that. Something out of a nightmare.

A creature driven by a rage like nothing else on Earth.

* * *

One Day Earlier...

In a small laboratory in the heart of the city, two young men were working their asses off. They were biochemists, both of them, and their surroundings reflected that. The room they were in was something of a biochemist's palace. Beakers and flasks filled with any compound one could imagine were available to them at all times, and all the equipment of their trade was there for the asking. Bunsen burners, microscopes, filtration thingies, all of the vital apparatuses of biochemistry could be found in plenitude. Perhaps too much plenitude. After all, they had seven Bunsen burners and only two people, which was sort of a weird waste of money. In any case, the men were well-equipped for the task they had been assigned. But it wasn't for want of supplies that they had hit their present difficulties.

"Four years of my life I've spent on this damn experiment," Hank Howard said, slicking back his long, dark hair, "and I have nothing to show for it."

Samuel Ellison, his colleague and oldest friend, looked up at him. Sam was a pretty generic white guy, short in height with short brown hair.

"Are you sure nothing's come out of it?"

Hank stared at the vial of fluid in his hands, and the pale green juice suspended within. His harsh, angry face stared back at him from the reflection in the glass. Sam waited for Hank's response, but none came.

"Earth to Hank, please come in."

Hank shook his head. "Sorry, did you say something?"

"Cripes, man, the whole world could blow up around you and you wouldn't even notice. You'd just be standing there with that dumb look on your face."

"Oh?" Hank shot back. "Well, hey, I always have to look at the dumb face *you* make when you read issues of *Musclebound Amazon She-Gladiators Monthly* on the clock."

"Touché," Sam said, with a click of his tongue.

"I'm sorry, Sam, it's just...I don't understand why it keeps turning blue."

"Did you try it on Billy?"

Hank looked over at the small cage which held the test rat. A small label on the cage read "BILLY." The label had never been changed, so all of the dozens and dozens of rats that Hank and Sam had worked on had been named Billy.

"I tell you, every time the serum turns blue, nothing happens to the rats."

"Sooo, it's about the color then."

"I can't say for sure. We don't have enough data still to say if that's the only variable." Hank rubbed his forehead again—he was starting to get a big vein bulging out on his temple, and in Sam's opinion it added a bad contour to his face. "God, four years and nothing solid."

"There you go, saying that nothing good has come out of this," Sam said.

"Just give me one good outcome," Hank moaned. He leaned down to inject Billy 236 with the bluish fluid in the needle.

A minute or two passed, and there were no results.

"You wanna talk about good outcomes?" Sam asked. "Let's see...how about Hannah? The girl with the great personality and the beauty to match."

"Well, yeah, of course that's good," Hank said. "But you know what I mean."

"Forget science for a minute. You know she's the best thing to happen to you in the last four years."

"Yeah, outside of these walls, she's the best thing to happen to me *period*," Hank agreed. "But Sam, our time here is running out. General Darwin has been more than gracious with our setbacks so far, but I don't think we can count on him to do so much longer."

"He should understand that Rome wasn't built in a day. This is harder than rocket science, you know." Sam was only half-joking with that remark.

"I'm no fool. I knew this would be complicated." Hank's face was very serious just then. "A serum to enhance the human body, heightening the immune system, increasing speed and strength—do you realize how long a human could live if we perfect this serum?"

"Trust me, I'm well aware of what this will mean for medicine. And I'm just as hungry to bring it to fruition as you are." Sam giggled nervously. "Sometimes I can't help but wonder if we're like the mad scientists of old, y'know, Vornoff and the others. 'Tampering in God's domain'...do you think *He's* the one stopping us?"

Hank wasn't one to believe in God, but with all of these struggles, he could certainly believe in the Devil.

"Damn it! I'm sick of failure!"

Just then, the two scientists heard a squeak from the cage—it was Billy the rat. Hank's heart started pounding. Could this be it...?

A purple cloud started billowing out from Billy's skin. This cloud was composed of deadly acid, and it soon dissolved his tiny body.

"Just like poor Billy 235 before him," Sam said sadly. "Maybe Billy 237 will be the hero we need."

Hank couldn't help but sink deeper into his brooding.

"You know, Hank, ever since we were kids, you've always been Mr. All Work and No Play." Hank turned to look at his friend. "It can drive you nutso, old pal. You need to have some more fun. Like, uh, thinking about when you're gonna pop the big question. Pretty girl like Hannah probably doesn't want to wait around, you know."

"I'm gonna do it *tonight*, man, I swear," Hank said. "I just...need to ask General Darwin's permission first." He sighed. "I know it's old-fashioned, but so is the General. I just don't want him going AWOL and terminating the experiment."

"And what if he says no? Are the two of you just gonna run off and elope?"

Hank rolled his eyes. "Get serious."

"Just don't be nervous! That man can smell your fear. He'll eat you for breakfast if he does that. Just look him in the eye and tell him how it's gonna be!"

"Easier said than done. I think I'd rather face a firing squad."

"Don't be such a Negative Nancy. I know Darwin's bad, but he can't be *that* bad."

Hank said nothing, deciding to let it go.

Perhaps he should be glad his friend didn't know how bad the General could get. Ignorance was bliss, after all.

* * *

"Ignorance! I will not tolerate ignorance!"

The aged walls of the expansive mansion trembled at the sound of their master's voice. The Darwin mansion was huge, but when General Jonathan Darwin got to yelling, there wasn't an inch of it his bellowing didn't reach.

"Sir! I'm sorry, sir!" exclaimed Wendy the maid.

The General marched across the library floor towards the hapless maid—he was clad in full field uniform, as though he was ready to ship out at a moment's notice. He trapped poor Wendy in the corner of the tall bookshelves, and then dramatically wiped his finger over the length of the shelves.

"What do you call this, soldier?"

"I-I..."

He blew the grayish powder that had collected on his fingertip into her face. "It's called dust, you imbecile. And I don't want it invading my home."

Darwin saw there was still some dust on his finger, so he wiped it off on Wendy's apron. Then, he folded his arms behind his back and started pacing.

"You let dust build up and before you know it, you've got an army of dust bunnies plotting to take over."

"Sir! I'm really sorry, General Darwin, sir!" Wendy *was* doing her best.

"Prove you're sorry! Drop and give me twenty!"

"I...what?"

"Do it! *Now!*"

Wendy felt like she was gonna have a panic attack. She didn't want to know what the consequences for failure were if the *threats* were this bad. She immediately hit the floor and started on her pushups.

There was no disrespecting the General in this house. Not one goddamn iota.

Outside, young Hank prepared himself for the meat grinder. Tonight was the big night, and he'd gone out of his way to put on the dog. The tuxedo and bowtie looked good on him, and his black pants were ironed and pressed. His shaking hands held a bouquet of roses. He'd parked his car cleanly behind the giant water fountain that stood outside the Darwin house, and now, he was waiting for someone to answer the call of the doorbell.

He was mumbling to himself.

"General Darwin, sir, I'd like to ask you for the privilege to marry your daughter." No, that wasn't firm enough. "General Darwin, sir, I love Hannah, and I want to prove my love by marrying her. Will you allow me?" Mm, too direct…

Hannah opened the door. Upon seeing her beauty Hank was all smiles—her long hair was a gorgeous dirty blonde, and it went well with her cornflower eyes. The cream-colored dress she was wearing looked perfect on her. He handed her the flowers.

"You look stunning, babe," he said.

She stepped forward and gave him the most smoldering kiss she'd ever handed out—which was saying something. Hank felt his cheeks flush red as summer tomatoes.

"Well, dang, I hope that's not how you greet the mailman!"

"Have you seen my mailman?" she laughed. "Blackmail couldn't make me kiss that frog."

Hank raised an eyebrow, contemplating for a moment the fact that the woman he wanted to make his wife was deeply prejudiced against the French. She spoke of this feeling only rarely, but when she did she was always passionately hateful, always breaking out that word, that spat curse, "frogs." She knew such biases weren't acceptable in today's world, so she kept it on the down-low—but as her boyfriend, Hank knew her secret.

"Come on in," she said. "Let me find some water for these flowers. I'll be back in a jiffy."

"Take your time," Hank said, his voice dropping low suddenly. "I have to talk to your father about something."

Once Hannah was out of sight, he retrieved the ring box from his pocket, and gazed once more at the glittering ring within.

Suddenly, Hannah's head became visible from around the corner.

"What are you gonna talk to Dad about?"

Hank's hands never moved faster than they did to conceal the ring.

"The experiment?" she added. By pressing her question, she had given him an out.

He took it. "Uh, yeah," he said. "There's some new data I want to discuss with him."

Hannah gave him a look—the kind of piercing look that showed that she was suspicious of him.

"Alright," she said, stretching the word. "I'll let you discuss your...data..."

Hank forced a smile. He wanted to get down on his knee and propose right that moment—but he knew he had to do things "right."

Once Hannah again slunk out of view, Hank went to go find the General. He knew that Darwin preferred hanging out in the library, and Hank had been there many times while rendezvousing with Hannah, so he knew the way.

When he entered the library, he found the General standing over a woman who he recognized as the maid, Wendy. She was doing one-handed push-ups, and was absolutely drowning in sweat.

"I want your last two *no*-handed!" the General barked.

"Sir! I-I can't do a no-handed push-up, sir!" Wendy blustered.

Just then, her strength gave out, and she flopped down on the library floor.

"Worthless!" Darwin cried. "Just like all the rest! On your feet!"

Wendy struggled to get up—it took her quite some time. Hank couldn't help but feel bad for her. She was in for a cashiering.

"You're a disgrace to the uniform!"

Darwin tore away Wendy's apron—she'd been drummed out of the corps. Clad only in her dress, Wendy left the mansion sobbing—never to return.

The General's face didn't waver for an instant. He never regretted his actions. After all, he was only doing his duty—he had to enforce the order that held this house together, and kept it a sturdy fortress against the tides of chaos. It was part of the responsibilities he possessed both as a father and as a servant of his country.

He turned towards Hank, who he had noticed but ignored.

"Well, what are you waiting for, soldier? Speak!"

"General Darwin, sir, it's good to see you," Hank said, thankful for the chance to speak at last. "I have to talk to you about something important."

"Ah, making progress with the experiment, are we?"

"This isn't about the experiment, sir. It's about—"

"Shh!"

The General swept up to him, placing a finger over his lips. "Not here, not here. These shelves could be bugged."

Hank raised an eyebrow. "Shall we…" And he pointed to the door to the wine cellar. The General nodded, and marched over to that door. The two descended the old wood stairs together, and soon found themselves surrounded by row upon row of wine racks, which were filled to the absolute brims with antique bottles. This collection alone must have cost more than the house. Distantly, Hank realized that this place was or had once been an old bomb shelter.

The General located an oaken barrel which he'd placed among the racks, which had a tap on it. Nearby was a stack of glasses. "A drink, Howard?"

"No, thank you, sir."

Darwin placed his glass under the tap and poured out two fingers worth. "I rarely drink on duty, but the discussion of this project merits some lapse in authority," he said. He took a long sip of the blood red liquid, and then he sighed.

"I need results, Howard. I need results, and I need them fast."

"Like I said, General, the experiment is going fine," Hank said. "I'd like to speak to you about Hannah for a moment."

Darwin frowned, and took another sip of his wine. "Hannah? What about her?"

"Sir, I—"

"Well, spit it out!"

Now Hank sighed.

"I love your daughter, sir, and I'd like to marry her."

"What?!"

"I-I said that I would like your permission to marry Hannah."

The General snorted derisively. "Did you knock my little girl up, you little pervert? Huh?"

"No! Hannah's not pregnant! I meant what I said, I *love* her. And I have for a long time."

"Ha! Love. Little civilian pissants like you always claim it's love. But I admire your guts, dirtbag. You answered well. I've always appreciated your brains—and the fact that you know how to use them."

Hank scowled, but swiftly repressed the expression. "Do I have your blessing to marry your daughter? Or not?"

Darwin only laughed. "You're kidding—you think I want a deadbeat son-in-law? Negative."

"Deadbeat?! What the hell are you talking about? I'm a scientist, the head scientist on your pet project."

"I want results! The government will stop funding this program unless you start showing some goddamn results! And until I see some, I sure as hell will not let you marry my daughter! Got it?"

Hank couldn't hold back his anger. His fists clenched—and as they did so, he felt something surge up inside him. It was like his rage was a living thing, separate from yet a part of him. It wanted vengeance—it wanted to destroy General Darwin.

"Just try and stop me," he growled.

He turned and left the wine cellar, not waiting for the General's dismissal. The General opened his mouth to shout something at him—but then he considered that it was no use.

"I've lost this battle," Darwin murmured, "but I will *not* lose the war."

He polished off his wine with a sharp slug from the glass.

As Hank stomped back up into the library, he found Hannah waiting for him. He strode past her before she could speak, saying only to her: "Let's go."

Hannah scoffed. It was clear Hank was in a mood—and she knew what that meant.

"Let me guess," she said, trying to keep pace with him. "The General said something you didn't like."

Hank didn't say anything. Instead, he simply pushed his way through the house's front doors, and led her to his car.

"I already told you, it's nothing. Now c'mon, I just wanna get out of here."

Hannah was offended, and didn't hide it. "Calm down, Hank. I don't it when you get all angry. It doesn't suit you."

They climbed into the car, and he slammed his door. "Just drop it, will you?"

She didn't conceal her rolling her eyes either. He saw it, and guilt was already rising up in him. Tonight was supposed to go better than this. Damn Darwin!

No matter what, he couldn't lose control of the storm of anger that seemed to rage inside him.

<h1 style="text-align:center">2.</h1>

Far away from the Darwin Mansion stood another fantastically massive estate. In the desert outside of the city an enormous castle blocked out the light of the full moon. It was the sort of castle one might find among the bourgeois vampire families of the Carpathians, all mossy black stone and spiked spires and gargoyles, and swooping halos of bats. The whole castle had been shipped across the Atlantic from Germany and reassembled, brick by brick. The expense of performing such a feat was incomparable. There was little doubt that whoever was master of this castle was a formidable presence indeed.

At the heart of this vast castle was the central control room. There were many other important chambers—the torture chamber, the biological experiments lab, the go-kart track—but the control room was the most important of all. It was full of monitors, which not only displayed images from all around the castle but from many places around the world as well. Landmarks like the Grand Canyon, the Golden Temple, and the Eiffel Tower, as well as places of government like the White House, the Rashtrapati Bhavan, and the Palais de l'Elysee, were visible upon these screens. One would think that a diplomat or world leader resided within this strange, ancient structure.

Instead, a young woman was dancing to classical music by some guy named Strauss. By "dancing," one must interpolate the word "twirling." She was twirling around and giggling, syncing her giggles somewhat in time with the music but mostly just making noise.

Lolita Schiller was noise in human form. Her pink shirt was loud, her curly blonde hair was loud, her enormous brown puppy-dog eyes were loud. And she was always moving around, dancing arrhythmically in nearly every moment of idleness. She had quite a lot of idleness in her life, having never had to work—some might go so far as to call her a spoiled brat, but that would just make her cry. Despite these questionable traits, she was decently pretty, and perhaps more significantly for the particular context which surrounded her life, she was very curvy. The door to the control room was guarded by two strong men, clad in the traditional garb of Roman legionnaires, and they were chuckling to themselves for the private show they were getting. That jiggly body and those dance moves were like chocolate and peanut butter.

Lolita's dance was suddenly interrupted by the appearance of a large, bulky figure. The purple-clad titan was a true ogre of a man, broad and heavy and stone-faced. Had he not chosen to stick out his bottom lip like a petulant child, he could have been truly fearsome. He supported himself on a long black lacquered cane, rather like those used by pimps in 1970s exploitation films, and a monocle covered one of his cruel, staring eyes. Somehow, Lolita had failed to notice the trademark klak-klak of the monstrous man's freshly-shined Italian shoes.

Those shoes *klak-klakked* again as their wearer marched over to the CD player that was playing the Strauss track. His ring-drowned finger flicked the accursed machine off. Lolita didn't get the hint—she had the groove going, and unless interrupted, she'd be dancing for hours. The large man cleared his throat and thumped his heavy cane against the floor once, twice, and *thrice*. That got her attention; she stopped dancing and turned half-startled to face him. Behind her, a small pug pup, Stanley, cowered in fear, for he knew what the big man was capable of.

Lolita wasn't afraid, though. She smiled at the man, and stepped up to kiss him warmly. To her, his wrinkled trollish lips were very heaven. She let behind a generous helping of her thickly applied lipstick.

"Pookie bear! Where have you been? I get so lonely waiting for you."

She strode over to one of the room's elegant wooden table, where she had placed her mani kit. She started doing her nails, though not before popping a piece of gum in her mouth and chewing it loudly.

The large man stared at the nail supplies derisively. "Vhat haff I varned you about?" he asked. His voice carried a resonant German accent.

Lolita didn't bother looking up from what she was doing. "What?" she asked.

He pointed the tip of his cane at the furniture she was using. "This table has been in the Kantlove family for centuries! And I, Dr. Werner von Kantlove, vill not see it desecrated by your spilled paints! Remove it! *Macht schnell!*"

"But bumblebee, I'm bored." Lolita made a mock sad face, a face she was so used to making that it no longer had any real emotion behind it. The expression soon melted, and she instead a pleasantly horny smile broke out across her lips. "Now that you're back, maybe we can have some fun…"

Dr. Kantlove rolled his eyes. "You should know you can't vin me over that way."

"Ohh, yeah, that's right, I forget. There's nothing going on…" and she pointed meaningfully between his legs, "…downstairs."

"And you ought to know too not to start vith that!"

Lolita seemed to understand that was a hit below the belt. Literally. "I'm sorry, Pookie. I didn't mean to hurt your feelings!"

"Hmph. You talk about my hurt feelings…vhat haff I told you

about gyrating in front of the guards? That is a big no-no vith me!"

He gestured to the two armor-clad castle defenders. He saw the lust in their cocky smiles, and scowled at it—which only made them grin wider.

He strode towards the two men menacingly. He prodded one of them with his cane. "Do you find something amusing?" Then, to the other man: "Do I look like...a clown...to you?"

A tiny bit of Lolita's lipstick had found its way onto the doctor's nose.

"No, sir, Dr. Can't-Love, sir!" the guard barked. As soon as the words escaped his mouth he cursed himself silently. "I mean, Kantlove, sir!"

Kantlove raised a gloved hand and slapped the guard firmly across the face. "Dummkopf!" He masked the pain he felt from striking the metal of the man's helmet.

The giant man turned away from the guards, and the man who'd been slapped raised his hand and flipped the bird. Stanley the dog spotted this and barked. As if comprehending the beast, Kantlove turned back and caught a glimpse of the fast-retreating hand.

"So! You like to make funny gestures when you zink ve are not looking!"

"Sir! I wasn't doing anything, sir!"

The impudence! "Stanley told me all about it," Kantlove hissed.

"You're going to believe a dog over me, sir?"

"I'm afraid that's how the cookie crumbles."

This time a slap wasn't enough. Kantlove moved to the computer console nearby and pressed a button. Suddenly, as if from nowhere, a beam of white-hot particles streamed out and struck the guard with enough energy to make his bones glow through his flesh. The flesh crumbled in ashy clumps away from the bones, and the skeleton stayed standing a moment longer before falling in pieces to the ground.

The surviving guard blanched, and crossed himself in the name of the Sacred Mother.

Kantlove sniffed with amusement. "Cookies aren't the only thing that crumble." And he turned back towards Lolita.

"Did we get the ransom money yet?" she asked excitedly.

Kantlove nodded triumphantly. "It vas transferred to the Sviss account moments ago."

All of Lolita's dreams had come true in an instant. "Shopping spree in Paris! Yippee!" She resumed her earlier dancing, only much more excitedly. But she stopped herself suddenly. A thought had occurred to her.

"Waaiiit...does this mean...?"

Kantlove's eyes lit up then, even more than they had when he mentioned the money.

"Oh, come on, Pookie, can we do it now?" Lolita exclaimed. "Please, Pookie, don't hold out on me. I need it!" She tilted her face down a bit, and made a face that was legitimately sensuous. "Give it to me!"

Kantlove smiled proudly and sat down at the control terminal. Then, he patted his lap gently. Lolita jumped onto him as if it were her first instinct in life.

"Tell me, my dear..." Kantlove began. "Vould you like something...*big*?"

"Oh, yes, Pookie!" Lolita cried.

"Vould you like something...*hard*?"

"Oh, *yes*, Pookie!"

"Vould you like something...*messy*?"

"Oh, yes, yes, yes!"

Kantlove's hand lifted a panel and exposed a big red button.

"Then vhy don't you go ahead, mein Liebling...and *take* vhat you vant?"

He started the Strauss music back up—and Lolita's hand slowly moved towards the button.

"I don't know if I can..." she giggled. "I want to...oh, I *want* to..."

"Then push the button," came Kantlove's whisper in her ear.

She gave in to her urges, and pressed the button down hard into the desk.

Castle Kantlove's rocket systems came to life, and a three-stage missile prepared itself for immediate launch. The guidance computer worked swiftly to track its target, and once it was locked the ignition countdown began.

Kantlove and Lolita counted together:

"Five…

"Four…

"Three…

"Two…

"One…

"Liftoff!"

The rocket ignited and its steely shaft started its climb towards the heavens. It hadn't been easy for the good doctor to get his hands on an ICBM, but it was doable in these days of the Internet. This missile was bound for Germany, the Kantlove clan's ancestral homeland. It was time to take care of an old grudge.

Kantlove's screens shifted to show a large brownstone building. The black chimneys spiking up from the roof suggested it had once been a factory, maybe for munitions. Inside were some of Germany's finest scientific minds.

If each of the people in that building had taken decades to build their genius, then there was centuries worth of knowledge contained in that building. But one second was all it would take to wipe it all out forever.

Lolita watched the missile's path on the radar in anticipation. Each mile it crossed built up more and more ecstasy within her.

"Almost there…" she said softly. "Oh God, it's almost there!"

The missile had crossed the Atlantic, and soon passed over Spain and France. It homed in on its target with the purpose and loyalty of a hunting dog.

"Almost there…!"

The rock dropped out of the sky, and before anyone in the

building could react, it exploded with a roar of noise and flame. The building and the people inside were reduced to only so much scattered dust.

Mixed in with the sound of the explosion was Lolita's ecstatic moan. One of her legs tensed and straightened, and she fell shuddering into Kantlove's arms.

Eventually, this quivering burst of joy passed, and she sat back up. "Ohh, there is nothing like that," she whispered.

Kantlove grinned, always glad to make his wife happy.

"That vill show them to mock my genius! Institute for the Advancement of German Scientists...bah! Laugh at Werner von Kantlove, vill they? Now I have all their money, and they have nothink...*nothink*!"

Lolita couldn't hide the fact that her lover's bloodlust fanned her ardor.

"Make love to me, Pookie, please. Just like how you used to."

"Ah, you stupid voman," Kantlove mused. "You know I am not able to perform in *zat* vay anymore."

Then he stood up, without warning, sending his paramour tumbling to the ground. "I must have mein pills. They take an hour to kick in. I cannot just jump into bed mitt you all...villy-nilly." He panted heartily. "You know I have mein condition!"

"Well, then..." She wrapped her arms around his neck. "Can you blow up another one? Pretty, pretty please?"

"Darlink, a man needs rest after a big explosion. I'm only human."

"But Pookie-sweetie-honey-darling..."

Kantlove couldn't resist how cute she was. He reached over to the controls, keeping his eyes on her the whole time. Another smile broke out across his face as he readied another salvo of missiles.

When Lolita saw how many he was arming, she almost shrieked with delight—she was a screamer when she got going. "Yes, Pookie, yes, yes!"

"Go, mein little curryvursts, go!" Kantlove cried. He once again slammed his hand on the ignition button.

Rockets blasted off left and right, seeking their targets.

Kantlove laughed insanely as he watched the unfolding catastrophe. The salvo pummeled all of the world's greatest monuments—so many of humanity's great wonders were blown to pieces. London Bridge: smashed! The Sphinx: crushed! The Great Wall of China: obliterated! The Taj Mahal: annihilated! The U.N. Building in New York: flattened! The United States Capitol: pulverized! The Lincoln Memorial: mangled! The Golden Gate Bridge: macerated! The Sydney Opera House: fractured! Mt. Rushmore: desolated! The Hollywood Sign: desecrated! Stonehenge: decimated! Machu Picchu: ravaged! The Roman Colosseum: wrecked! The White House: ruined! The St. Louis Arch: well, you get the idea.

Kantlove laughed, even as Lolita howled in ecstasy. Some men want to please their wives, others just want to watch the world burn. The doctor had the best of both worlds.

His laughter grew weaker and weaker, until he cut it off with a cough. "I think that's enough for now, Liebchen."

"No!" Lolita screamed happily. "More, more, *more!*"

He waved his hand at her weakly. "Go play. Go play mit your toys." It was clear he was done for the night.

The young woman made a pouty expression—she was utterly insatiable. But she figured this was good enough, for now.

She turned towards the far corner of the room—she'd left her hula hoop over there, and went to go retrieve it. When she picked it up, however, she saw that a bite had been taken out of it—now it was less a hula hoop than a hula line.

"Stanley!" she cried. "How many times have I told you not to chew on my stuff!"

She threw down the broken toy and walked over to where the disintegrated guard's bones were. She picked up his femur and lifted it up before an interested Stanley.

"Go fetch!" she said, and threw the bone away.

The bone spun mesmerizingly through the air as it sailed towards the far end of the room. It was hard to say who was more fascinated by the sight, Lolita or the dog.

3.

There are few experiences in this world lovelier than a carnival at night. The flashing lights, the warm glow of the games, the smell of the fried food...it was more than enough to scrape away the tensions that had arisen between Hank Howard and Hannah Darwin. The young couple remembered why they were in love— they both loved life, and all the excitement it could bring. They rode all the roller coasters, and won all the prizes for each other at the games. They were happy. And that was exactly what Hank needed if he was going to propose.

All throughout the night, the thought stayed at the back of his mind that he had to keep an eye out for the moment where Hannah was at her happiest. That was the exact moment when he would strike. Of course, it would be convenient if that happiest moment could happen somewhere where there were few people around—but somehow Hank didn't care about anyone else tonight. The whole world was just an illusion next to the love he had for Hannah. Tonight was the night. He could feel it.

It looked the Ferris wheel was gonna provide the joy Hank was looking for. Hannah had ridden a lot of Ferris wheels as a kid, and greatly missed the experience as an adult. And so there was a genuine wonder in her eyes as they rose up high above the bright lights of the carnival and she saw things as the birds saw them.

When they came back down, she said, "I didn't know I could still feel that way. I thought I grew out of things feeling that good." Her smile made Hank's heart sing.

She wanted to go on another roller coaster next, and he obliged her. There wasn't really a good place to have the talk by the Ferris wheel anyway. Still, he figured now was the time to put his foot in the door. He had to set things up.

They were getting loaded onto the coaster when he said, "Hannah...when we're done with this one, there's something I gotta ask you."

"What is it?"

"I—"

An employee came by and said hurriedly, "Raise your arms." He was walking down the coaster clicking everyone's bars into place. Hank held back what was he going to say until the man was gone.

"Hannah, I—"

"What were you gonna say?" she interrupted.

God, just let say it, he thought to himself. "I wanted to talk to you about—

"Hold on tight!" the ride operator shouted, and just then, the coaster jolted forward. As it gained speed, the young couple got nervous. Hank forgot his words, and underneath the bar that kept them in place the lovers grabbed each other's hands.

"Oh, Hank, this one looks really scary..."

"I wish I hadn't eaten that chili dog before the Ferris wheel..."

And suddenly, they were off, at speeds that Hank thought were only possible within a laboratory centrifuge.

Somehow, though, he didn't spill his guts. It was like he didn't notice the speed, or the drops, or the hairpin turns after a point. He was lost in that pre-proposal anxiety that anyone who's gotten engaged knows about.

He was getting tired of going on rides. But his patience was paying off. This coaster seemed intense enough for Hannah—it drove the urge out of her. There weren't too many rides left to go on, anyway, and they had already had all the funnel cake they could eat. So once they were back on the ground, he tried to talk her into going on a walk.

"How 'bout a stroll...to the train? To get back to the car?" came her reply. "I'm beat, babe, I want to go home."

"Fair enough," he said, feeling some small measure of defeat.

"Let's take the subway," she suggested. "I always thought subways are so romantic."

He grinned at that.

In no time at all they were aboard a subway car, being whisked off into the great unknown. Or at least, off towards where the car was parked. Hannah had a point, there was something strangely romantic about the glint of fluorescent light off of old battered steel. The smell in the air wasn't great, but there was artistic value to be found in some of the graffiti on the wall.

Hank knew the clock was ticking. This night had been as torturous as it was wonderful. He loved being around Hannah, and seeing her happy, but he didn't want this moment to slip away from him. Maybe what he was about to do was too random, too inappropriate, but suddenly he didn't care. Love was about spontaneity after all, and so he sucked in a deep breath and went for it.

"Hannah, I really have to ask you something."

"That's what you said on the coaster, too. What is it? Just tell me."

He took her hand.

"Baby, we've been through a lot over the last four years. And—"

"Y-yes?"

"Well, I wanted to know—"

Hannah's eyes lit up.

But not in delight. "Look out!" she cried.

Hank spun around, and saw himself standing before a tall, grubby man in a dark coat. The man's face was twisted into an ugly leer. In his hand was a small pistol.

"Hank, be careful," Hannah whispered. They both raised their hands in the air.

It's ironic, Hank considered. *A few minutes ago we were raising our hands to feel the wind on the coaster. Now we're raising them to save our lives.*

"Move a muscle and you two bitches are dead," the man said. "Now give me your wallet."

Hank hesitated.

"Do what he says, Hank."

"Your lady's got more sense than you do!" He pressed the gun tight into Hank's ribs. "Come on, give!"

Hank could feel his anger surge up in him. He had to protect the ring. He would turn over his wallet, but not that.

"Here," he said, producing the wallet. "All the cash in here is all yours. Now take it and leave."

"Well, I'm a lucky man tonight, it seems," the robber chuckled. "But I like those earrings you got too, sweet thing. Hand 'em over before I rip 'em out of your ears!"

Hannah sighed contemptuously and removed the earrings, handing them over to the thief.

"Okay, you got what you wanted," Hank growled. "Now fuck off, won't you?"

The mugger only laughed.

"You're not in any position to tell me what to do. I wanna see what else you got."

Just then, Hank's heart quickened, for the crook's hand was snaking into the pocket where he was keeping the ring box.

"And what do we have here?"

That was enough. Hank swung his fist straight at the robber's head. The man was surprised, not expecting such a violent gesture. He blocked the punch with the hard metal of his gun. Then, with his free hand, he slammed a punch of his own into

Hank's ribs. Hank groaned, and the ring box toppled free of his pocket. The mugger stooped down low and swept it up, and then dashed off towards the car doors. The train had started slowing for the platform a few moments ago, and the timing couldn't be worse. Hank chased the man out of the open doors but he was already lost in the crowd that was swarming around the platform.

The scientist's heart sank. He had worked so hard to buy that ring, and now it was lost.

"Hank! Are you hurt?"

Hank turned back to face Hannah. She ran forwards and hugged him tight. As she pressed up against his rib he coughed a little, and she pulled back.

"It's okay. Nothing's broken," he said. "I'll be alright."

"Why in God's name would you pull a stunt like that?" she asked. "What was in your pocket that was worth risking your life for?"

Hank knew that he couldn't tell the truth—it would be so sloppy of him to fumble the proposal by telling her that some asshole had run off with the diamond ring he'd spent years saving for. He was worried she would blame him for failing to get it back, even though she had just gotten upset at him for risking his life. So he lied.

"It was a flash drive with some important documents for the experiment. Top secret stuff. If it fell into the wrong hands, there's no telling what could happen."

"Well, I doubt that a mugger would find that very useful. I'd be shocked if the creep could actually read."

"I guess I overreacted. It was stupid, I know."

"I'm just glad you didn't get killed!"

Hank smiled at that. He had felt for so much of the night that he was losing her love—but it was clear right now that she was concerned for him.

"What do you say we call it a night, huh?" he said.

"That's a good idea," she replied gently.

They left the sub station and found their way back to Hank's car. The long drive back to Hannah's house was a silent one. The night was cold and the wind had a mocking tone to it.

When they pulled up in front of the Darwin Mansion, Hank said, "I'll call you tomorrow morning."

"Whenever you get up," Hannah said. "You might want to sleep in after what happened tonight."

"Sleep can wait. I'm gonna drive over to the lab and put in some hours tonight."

Hannah's eyes widened. "What? Honey, you gotta get some rest. Your health is more important than some dumb experiment."

"Your father told me the government is threatening to stop funding the project. Unless I can get some results soon, it's over."

Disappointment clouded her face. "Oh...so that's why you've been so moody lately."

"Can't you see that this project means a lot to me? And to your father?"

"Fine." Her tone was bitter again. "Go to the lab and do whatever you want. I'm outta here."

She opened the car door and stormed out into the night. Hank raised a hand.

"Hannah, wait!"

But it was too late. She reached the front door to the house and threw it open, and then, with a loud slam, she passed into the house and disappeared.

Hank's face darkened. He had to get to the lab. It was time to finish this.

4.

For hours Hank toiled in the lab, alone. The rest of the building was dark and empty; Sam wasn't by his side, as he always was. That was just how Hank wanted it—this was personal. This was something for him and him alone to finish, no one else. And he would do it tonight. He had no idea how, but he had a few clues in the right direction. One by one he mixed the formulas together and injected them into the test organisms. One by one he saw his trials end in failure.

He couldn't give up—his marriage to Hannah was on the line. He tried to let love guide him to success, but as the night wore on and the disappointment piled up, he began to find that rage was a stronger motivator. He started thinking less of his love for Hannah and more about his fury against General Darwin for denying their engagement. He wanted to prove that dumb old man wrong. He wanted to conquer him, beat him once and for all so that he and Hannah could be happy together at last. The General was at the heart of so much of Hank's suffering, and the hate he felt for him seemed to consume the whole of his spirit.

Now he was mixing the latest of the two compounds together. It was nearly 3 in the morning, and the exhaustion of three hours' work weighed heavily on him.

"So the General wants results, huh?" he murmured. "Then results I'll give him."

As the two liquids merged in the beaker, something surprising happened—it was even more amazing than the time the formula turned blue. This time, it turned *purple*. He had never seen that before.

"Purple..." he whispered. "Maybe...maybe it could work..."

His latest test subject was a dead flower—in fact, it was one of the flowers which he given Hannah earlier in the night. He poured a sample of the new serum onto its withered petals.

Three minutes ticked by. If the formula worked then it should've worked faster than that.

"Another failure! That's the story of my life."

But just then, something began to change. Slowly, the flower began to stir back to vitality. The faded crimson flushed a deep red, and the petals stiffened as the formula rehydrated them.

"I can't believe it. It worked!" The plant cells had been revitalized and restrengthened! "It really worked!"

He was ready to start celebrating, but just then he frowned.

"This isn't enough!" he exclaimed. "Just not enough. This would've been great maybe two years ago—but right now I need *bigger* results. And not tomorrow...today!"

In that moment, the last of Hank's mental defenses shattered. His inhibitions melted away, and suddenly the path ahead seemed so clear. It was crazy, of course—at least, that's what he would've said, were he in his right mind. But the robbery tonight had pushed him over the edge. That mugger had pushed him around just like the General had. And Hank was tired of being the universe's punching bag.

Maybe he didn't even care if what he was about to do killed him.

He drew out a few milligrams of the purple liquid from the beaker, and then slowly moved the syringe towards his arm. Sweat beaded on his skin, and he saw that he was shaking. No matter. He had to give it a try.

"Here goes," he said softly.

And then he drove the needle into his arm and pushed the plunger.

Suddenly the needle dropped from his hand, shattering against the floor. "My God…" Hank cried suddenly. "What have I done?"

A savage pain flooded through his body in an instant—a burning, tingling sensation. It was like being dragged over a bed of hot coals. Hank couldn't hold back his scream.

Then the burning shifted into something else, a crackling sort of pain. The fire that burned within him had turned into a raging thunderstorm. He could feel terrible forces swelling and condensing inside him, and he wondered just what the hell was going to happen.

Was this death? Was this the end?

It had to be. It hurt so bad, and this electrical feeling…

It was like being carried away on a wild mustang. It was like flying off into the dark night.

And then, for Hank Howard…all went blank.

* * *

Hours later, at the castle in the desert, Dr. Kantlove was sitting in his office examining the latest trinket his men had brought him. A glittering diamond ring sparkled between his gloved fingers. He was examining it closely with a jeweler's glass, and his knowledge of chemistry enabled him to confirm it was a real diamond.

Across from his desk sat two of his henchmen, dressed in their armor. They were both grinning proudly, for they had clearly impressed their boss, which was a difficult feat to achieve.

"And vhere did you say you two found this again?"

The two men started excitedly chattering over each other, but the doctor waved his hands.

"Vun at a time, please, vun at a time!"

He gave the nod to the man on his left, arbitrarily. The man started speaking:

"We were in the city taking care of some business, and we ran into your old chum Scully."

"Ah, yes, Scully," Kantlove said slowly, chewing the scenery with each word. "He owes me quite a bit of green now, doesn't he?"

The man on Kantlove's right burst in: "Yessir! Y'see, sir, Scully started—"

"Hey!" barked the first man. "I'm the one tellin' this story."

"You never let me get a word in edgewise anymore. What's up with that?"

"Hey, tough potatoes, man."

"Listen, you son of a—"

"Enough!" Kantlove cried, slamming his fist on his desk. "Enough! Just tell me vhat happened!"

The first man went on.

"As I was saying, we ran into Scully in the city. We decided to remind him of his debt, and told him he had to pay right then and there. Then I asked him how he'd like to take a little swim. With cement slippers!"

"You didn't say that," the second man said, "I did. That was *my* one-liner."

"Okay, fine, he said it. Anyway, what matters is, Scully decided this was his way of paying what he owes." The proud storyteller pointed to the ring. "You like that, boss?"

"I think that Lolita vill like it very much," Kantlove mused. "It vill make a lovely present for her. I just have vun question."

"Yeah, boss?"

"Vhat vas that you threatened Scully vith? You said you offered him...a little svim?"

"I said that, boss," the second man.

"I like that very much," Kantlove laughed. "Very much indeed. A little svim. That's clever..."

"Yeah, I just—I like to do a little improv sometimes, boss."

"Vell, you've certainly got the knack for it."

"Thank you, Dr. Can't-Love, sir."

At once, the man blanched. The fatal Freudian slip had touched yet another of the good doctor's men.

"I-I'm sorry, sir, I mean…"

"I think you should put your svimming trunks on," Kantlove said angrily, "because *you* are going for a little svim."

"No, no, Dr. Kantlove, please!"

Two more guards appeared suddenly, and grabbed the offender by his shoulders. "Take him away!" Kantlove cried, with a laugh.

The remaining man, the storyteller, looked absolutely petrified. He quietly snuck out of the room when the diamond ring once again took over Kantlove's focus.

***

Hours after that, the morning came, and Hank Howard woke up.

Confusion loomed over him from the first moment. He wondered immediately how he had gotten back home to his apartment. He didn't remember leaving the lab last night, but he was here now, so he must've taken off shortly after the thing with the flower. And he was so tired his brain had erased the memory of the drive home. And yet—when he looked out his bedroom window, he didn't see his car out front.

He'd had some weird dreams. A blur of images, half-remembered glimpses of the night before, haunted him—he saw the city at night, with its lights nearly as bright as the ones at the carnival. He saw rain, rain pouring down, rain running all the colors of the city together like the pigments of a melting painting. And then—a glimpse of a woman, pretty like Hannah, walking down the street. A man, following her. The roar of a gun, the smell of gunpowder. And a scream, and a sound like the crunching of bone…

And through it all, a purple monster...a grape-colored behemoth whose body seemed to bulge and swell and pulsate.

Ugh, what a nightmare. But it wasn't as bad as everything that had come before. He had lost the ring. And with it, he had lost so much of his hope for a future with Hannah.

A knock at his door interrupted his thoughts. At once he tensed up—he wasn't expecting anyone.

"Hello?" called a man's voice. "Anyone home?"

"Hold on, I'm coming!" he said.

"Open up!" shouted a woman then. "It's the police!"

"Okay, okay!"

Hank sprinted to the door—if it was the cops, then there wasn't time for him to put on a shirt. He looked down at this chest, and something caught his eye. There was a stain on his pale skin, near to the black stripes of the jagged-edged tattoo that criss-crossed the flank of his torso. It was the stain of a strange purplish fluid.

Never mind that. He licked his thumb and wiped some of the fluid off, before completing his trek to the front entrance.

He opened the door, and found himself standing before a tall bald man and a serious-faced dark-haired woman.

"You guys really are cops," Hank said.

"Well, we ain't Ed McMahon with a big-ass check," the bald man said.

"What's—what's wrong, officers?" Hank asked, sheltering the purple stains in the shadow of the doorframe. "How can I help you?"

"Hi, Mr. Howard. I'm Lisa Tuttle, this is my partner Ray Garton," the woman said. "I'm sorry, did we wake you up?" Though her face was harsh, Hank got the immediate impression that she was the Good Cop of the typical Good Cop/Bad Cop dynamic.

"It's no problem, really," he said, "I overslept anyway."

"Well, if you're Henry Howard, we wanted to give you your wallet back."

The bald man, Garton, held up the wallet. Right before he handed it back, he took out Hank's license, and said, "Date of birth?"

"Can I just have that back, please?" Hank asked.

Tuttle elbowed Garton in the rib. "He's just kidding," she insisted. Garton sighed and replaced the card, and handed Hank the wallet.

"Thanks for delivering this," Hank said. "Honestly, I never thought I'd see it again. Where'd you find it?"

Garton smirked. "A better question is, how'd you lose it?"

"Uh, well...actually, I was mugged last night." Hank knew he had to choose his words carefully.

"That so?" Garton asked.

"Yeah, I was out with my girlfriend. We were on the subway when some guy robbed us at gunpoint."

Tuttle looked concerned. "Were either of you hurt?"

"No, luckily we weren't. But he took this, and my girlfriend's jewelry. And..." He paused a moment. "And he took the ring I was going to propose to her with."

"Aw, that's a bummer," Garton said, with a hint of authenticity in his voice.

"Did you file a report or anything?" Tuttle asked.

"It was late and we were tired. We didn't have the chance." He bit his lip. He knew he shouldn't ask this question, but he felt he had to. "Where—where did you find this again?"

Garton seemed eager to answer. "There was a double homicide last night," he said. "Near the old Mason Theater. A prostitute and a mugger were found dead in an alley. Guess which one of 'em had your wallet?" A smile crossed his face that filled Hank with fear.

"I-I..."

The crunch of bones...

"What's 'a matter, kid? Something wrong?"

Hank shook his head.

"Yeah, I'm okay," he said shakily. "It's just a lot. I mean, I'm still getting over being mugged in the first place, so it's damn weird to hear that the guy who did it killed a hooker and then ended up dead."

Garton raised an eyebrow at that. Hank wished cops weren't so persecutory.

"Well, you've been through a lot in the last 24 hours," Tuttle said, "and I don't think you need us hassling you, that's for sure."

No shit, Sherlock, Hank thought to himself. "Th-thank you so much for bringing over the wallet. I really, really appreciate it."

"Don't mention it," said Lisa Tuttle cheerily. "Take care, Mr. Howard."

She reached out and shook his hand. Though he was afraid of him, Hank realized he should the same for Garton. When their two palms touched, however, Garton once again raised his eyebrow. Hank didn't know that Garton felt something odd in that handshake.

"Goodbye, officers," he said.

"See you around, kid," said Garton. And he smirked. He knew no one wanted to hear a cop say that.

Hank closed the front door, and then turned and pressed his back against it hard. He let out a long sigh of relief, and sank slowly to the floor.

He had a sinking feeling that that dream was not a dream.

He kept thinking about that last detail of the dream. The howling purple giant.

He thought about the purple fluid in the test tube last night.

His head started spinning.

* * *

Outside of Hank's apartment, the two detectives were sitting in their car. Garton looked like the cat that swallowed the cream, or the canary, or something else of equal appeal to a cat's taste. Tuttle couldn't help but notice the cocky pride on his face.

"Okay, what gives?" she asked. "That Howard guy seems to have really tickled your pickle."

"Why, whatever do you mean, my darling?" Garton asked, sarcastically.

"Don't play coy with me, Ray. I can read you like a book." She sniffed. "You think you know something I don't, don't you?"

Garton only laughed.

"Come on, spill the beans, or I'll break out the third degree," she laughed back.

Suddenly Garton was a portrait of seriousness.

"I think our Henry Howard murdered that mugger."

"What?!" Tuttle spat. "You kidding? That guy seemed sweet. He doesn't look like he could even cheat on his income taxes."

"There are two pieces of evidence, my dear," Garton said.

"I'm listening."

"How come our sweet and innocent little Henry knew that the mugger killed that prostitute?"

"That...is a little weird, now that you mention it. But maybe he guessed, it's a pretty basic deduction. What else?"

Garton didn't answer for a long time.

"C'mon, spit it out, will ya?"

The suspense went on long enough. Garton raised his hand, the one he'd shaken Hank's with.

"That's—that's more of the purple stuff."

"Yeah. And it sure didn't come from the peanut butter and jelly sandwich I had for lunch."

Lisa Tuttle raised an eyebrow.

"I guess we have a trap to lay..."

5.

A couple hours later, Hank emerged from his apartment. He'd been seeking aspirin for the headache he'd developed after the night before, and found that he was completely out.

The two cops were watching him closely as he walked down the street towards the local Quickee Mart.

"It's showtime," Garton said.

As Hank passed through the door, the cashier greeted him, as was demanded by Quickee Mart corporate policy.

"Hey, dude, I'm—" And he glanced down to read his own nametag. "I'm Matthew, ha. But my friends call me Stoney. Like, welcome to the Quickee Mart, dude."

"Thanks, Stoney," Hank muttered. Stoney was, as his nickname suggested, perpetuated stoned, and so he forgot that Hank came into this store all the time. Stoney had "introduced" himself to Hank about eighty or ninety times.

Hank started his search for the aspirin. As he perused the shelves, he passed by the slushy machine. A teen was trying to pick a flavor from it.

"Wow, grape!" he exclaimed. "What a rare flavor to find on a machine like this!"

He poured the purple slush down into his cup. Hank

shuddered—the color reminded him of the stain he'd found. He kept thinking about that roaring purple monstrosity which haunted his nightmare...

He couldn't find the aspirin fast enough. His head was *throbbing*.

He got in line for the counter. There was only one person in front of him, an old lady. She was buying some denture cleaner. Why they sold that a convenience store, he had no idea, but he guessed it fit the label of "convenient."

"That'll be...ten sixty two, ma'am," Stoney said slowly.

"Let me see if I have exact change," the lady said. "I always like to give exact change."

She opened her purse, and slowly began to probe its contents for the right money.

She found a ten dollar bill but the coins were tripping her up. She found a quarter, and then two dimes, and took some time to add up what those were. Then she searched for another dime, or maybe two nickels...

Hank clenched his fist. *C'mon, hurry up, you old bag*, he thought.

"I may have to give you three quarters," she said, "but that's thirteen cents' change, that's bad luck. Let me keep looking."

Stoney didn't care. He was thinking about going home and smoking up in front of the PS3. Hank spotted a tiny speck of drool escaping the corner of his mouth.

Oh my God, this lady is driving me crazy! If she isn't done in two seconds, I swear I'm going to rip her limb from limb. Then I'm gonna use her severed arms to beat the shit out of that punk Stoney!

He knew he was kept more mad than the situation called for. He could've just opened the aspirin and taken some—he was gonna pay for it anyway. But the anger just kept swelling, creating an unbearable pressure.

"Fifty-nine cents..." the old lady gibbered, "sixty...sixty-one..."

"I can't stand it anymore!"

Once again, the storm burst out of Hank's body. It had happened before, but he had forgotten—this time, he was aware of what was happening. He could feel his flesh bulge and swell, surging with power. His muscles burst up huge under his skin, pushing through his white t-shirt and ripping it apart.

Hank knew he had to stop whatever was happening—his will pushed against the transformation, like he was sucking in his gut. He resisted the rage and drove his flexing muscles back to their normal size.

But his clothes were shredded. And now the old lady and the kid at the slushy machine and Stoney were all staring at him. The old lady was checking out his exposed chest a little bit.

He ran out of the Quickee Mart, scared as all hell. He had no idea what was happening to him.

The test. It had to be because of the test...

He remembered...

He'd injected himself with the compound.

He had to get back home. He had to figure out what had happened—

No. Home wouldn't have the answers he needed.

The alleyway, with the dead hooker. That was where he had to go.

He took off in the direction of that alley, homing in on it somehow, like he'd been there before. That was exactly what he was afraid of: that he had been there before.

He had no idea that Garton and Tuttle were right on his tail. His ripped shirt and his speed-walk flagged him as guilty in their eyes. And once he returned to the scene of the crime...well, there was an old police saying that went with that.

* * *

The chalk outlines of the two bodies jarred Hank pretty bad. They cemented the reality of the situation to him: two people were dead, and he was on record as having a motive for killing one of them. He felt sick inside.

There were other marks on the ground besides the body lines. There was also a strange gooey substance which, like the stains on his body, was a rich purple in color.

Now he was remembering something—the hot sting of bullets...

No—it was impossible. It couldn't be!

If someone shot at him, he couldn't just...take the bullets and live! But now the memories were coming back...memories of being shot...and surviving—

But he bled. He bled—purple.

He bled purple.

Like the formula.

He had been trying to tell himself that the purple beast he saw in his dreams was its own creature, its own entity. But now he could see the truth.

Hank's knees gave out under him, and though he hadn't eaten much more than a couple of aspirin, he threw up all over the pavement.

He felt tears of remorse well up in his eyes.

"Lose your lunch, kid?" came a familiar voice behind him.

Hank stood and spun around, and found the two police officers standing before him. Garton, who had spoken, once more bore a smug look on his face.

"This isn't what it looks like," Hank said.

Tuttle raised a reassuring hand. "Relax, Henry, everything is gonna be okay."

Hank was shaking. His whole body was trembling. He felt cold.

"What's the matter, kid?" Garton asked. "We're not gonna hurt you."

Hank couldn't stand it. He knew they were going to arrest him. And why shouldn't they?

He had killed that robber. He remembered now.

The mugger had found the prostitute soon after he had gotten done robbing him and Hannah. Hank had interrupted his attack on the hooker. But not as himself. As that monster...

And he had scared the thief so bad that his gun went off in the hooker's mouth. The back wall of the alley was streaked with gore. The murder horrified Hank, and his rage completely consumed him. He reached out for the mugger...

And he broke him like he was just a matchstick.

He was a monster. A giant purple monster.

A hairless titan whose great muscles shifted and undulated like purple Jell-O...

The experiment had ruined him. Darwin had ruined him!

And now these cops were gonna drag him to jail.

He couldn't stand it anymore. He had nothing left. And so he gave in to the raging storm that swirled within his heart.

A tornado seemed to form up around him, swallowing his body. Below those churning winds, his body once again swelled up and bulged. He gained height and weight and mass—great heaping tons of it.

The winds parted, and in Hank's place was the monster of his nightmares.

He was no longer Hank Howard—he was the Amazing Bulk!

Tuttle and Garton drew their weapons.

"What the hell is what?!" Tuttle howled.

"Well, it ain't Barney the Purple Dinosaur!" Garton exclaimed.

The Bulk wriggled his enormous muscles at them menacingly. He let out a roar that shattered the windows of the buildings around them.

"We'll have to call for backup!" Lisa said.

"Call for *backup*? It's gonna take an army to bring down that monster!"

The Bulk started approaching the two officers, and at once they could see he was nearly triple their size. He could stomp them into mashed potatoes without breaking a sweat.

But that's not what he was here to do. His first impulse was not to kill, but to get away.

He stomped right past the two officers, making a beeline for the open street. Then he hung a left and dashed down the street.

The two detectives had a duty to the public. They had to stop that nightmare before it was too late!

At once, they gave chase. The creature was still in sight by the time they rounded the corner—with his great size, it's not like he was able to hide anywhere. Garton and Tuttle took aim and opened fire.

The bullets had inconsistent effects. Sometimes they would bounce off from the thick purple hide harmlessly, like so many grains of rice. Sometimes they would puncture the skin, sending splatters of purple goo onto the pavement and provoking a pained roar from the titanic thing.

Those enormous legs, thick as an elephant's, sometimes impacted the cars that were parked on the streets—with the lightest brush he sent them catapulting through the air. They slammed down like missiles onto the sidewalk, shattering it into splintered mosaics.

At least there were no civilians in the way to get hurt. "Thank God it's Sunday!" Tuttle exclaimed, panting. "These streets would be full of people tomorrow!"

"Where the hell's that backup?!" Garton snarled.

Little did the detectives know that the entire police department, along with 90% of the city's citizenry, were at the ribbon-cutting ceremony for the opening of a new Bunkin' Bonuts Coffee and Donuts Franchise Shop. The police attendance at the ceremony only cost the taxpayers $36.7 million, which was much thriftier than last year's union-busting party.

Despite the relative emptiness of the city, word was spreading rapidly of what was happening. It was hard to miss the sound of smashing glass and screaming metal as cars, lampposts, phone booths, and anything else unfortunate enough to get in the Bulk's way were flung wildly through the air. Suddenly, a slow news day abated, and the local news station's flagship chopper was on the scene, eager for a buck to make.

The cameraman, Barry, leaned over the edge of the cockpit. The Bulk was gaining speed as he ran, and it was hard to keep him in the shot.

"I need a closer view!" he called to the pilot, Lyndon. "Bring us down a little bit!"

"Closer?" Lyndon yelled, over the roar of the blades. "Are you nuts? I have no idea what that thing down there is, and I sure as hell don't want to find out!"

Barry rolled his eyes. "Are you telling me you want to miss out on the scoop of the century? Are you telling me you want to miss out on the *payday* that comes with the scoop of the century?"

"You mean we could someday work for..." Lyndon didn't know if she could let herself reach this high. "...public access?"

"Yeah, we'll leave this shitty town and its shitty news

behind." Barry didn't care that his words were ending up on the recording.

"For freedom, then!" Lyndon yelled.

"For freedom! Yippee-ki-yi-yay!" Barry cried.

Lyndon angled the chopper down towards the Bulk, and swooped in low.

Neither of the reporters had noticed, however, what the two detectives on the ground had been observing. As the Bulk ran through the streets, he was getting bigger and bigger. He had started out about eighteen feet tall. Now he could reach the third or fourth story of the skyscrapers he sprinted past.

"You were right!" Lyndon laughed, ignorant of the danger. "We're gonna make history with this footage!"

"We gotta get closer!" Barry said. "We gotta get the mon-ay shot!"

"I-I don't want to get *too* much lower, though..."

"C'mon, girl, just a few more feet. Can't you see the headlines? 'Handsome Genius Reporter and Daredevil Lady Pilot Capture It All!'"

"Heh, you're right, I like the sound of that. Let's get in on that action…"

Just then, the Bulk had a growth spurt.

Suddenly, he was big enough to make King Kong look like the stereotypical but historically inaccurate portrayals of Napoleon. Now the roar of the copter blades was like the buzz of mosquitoes in his ear.

He spun around, and his huge arms lashed out towards the two journalists. They screamed as his enormous fingers wrapped their vehicle in a tight cage, one so firm that it stopped the spinning blades from moving. Purple blood from where the blades had struck his hands trickled over the doomed helicopter.

With a slight effort, the Bulk closed his hands into fists—crushing the chopper and the two riders within.

Ray Garton stared in horror—the monster had killed again. And now he was like a colossus, higher than the skyline itself. There was no stopping something like that.

Yet the Bulk still yearned only to escape. His started running again, his feet thundering over the road.

One of his toes snared another car, and threw it up into the air. Garton watched its trajectory, still paralyzed by terror.

Then he paled—he saw where the car was going to hit.

"Oh my God…*Lisa*!!"

Tuttle was still running after the Bulk, firing from what had to be her third or fourth clip. She had no idea what was happening until it was too late…

She looked up at the last second.

"Wha—?!"

She didn't feel a thing—she was dead before she could even finish processing it.

"*Lisa!!!*" Garton screamed. "*Nooo!!*"

He ran over to the smashed car, which was sitting in a pool of Lisa's blood.

His eyes were wide with horror—tears streamed down his cheeks. He was shaking.

But he was a cop. First and foremost.

His eyes slowly rose from his partner's battered corpse. They locked onto the purple titan who was speeding off into the distance. He was swiftly losing mass and volume, shrinking back down to his old size.

Garton continued the chase. He would carry on until Lisa was avenged.

As for the Bulk, pain and exhaustion were at last proving to be his downfall.

He was nursing several wounds from where the bullets had pierced him, and his hand really did smart from grabbing onto those helicopter blades. Plus, it took a lot of energy to move a body like that. He had to overcome the cube-square law and all other kinds of bothersome rules of physics.

As the Bulk faded away, Hank Howard returned. His mind slowly bloomed back to life within the Bulk's skull. His body continued to shrink, and as it reached a certain smallness it began to de-purple-ize as well.

Hank's thoughts swirled with confusion. The last few minutes had been like a fever dream to him, a cacophony of loud noises and screams and blurred images.

His clothes were now naught but rags, and there were bruises where the bullets had pierced him. His body was heavy and hung loose, like a puppet without strings. He was standing in an alleyway, and he staggered out of it into the bright sun.

He looked around, and saw the fires and the scattered rubble. It was enough to make his knees buckle for a moment.

Then Garton caught up to him. At last.

"You son of a bitch," he said. His face was covered with dust and his suit was torn. He still had his pistol, though. He raised it to Hank's face and, without a moment's hesitation, pulled the trigger.

Hank's eyes squeezed shut in an instant, dreading his death. But instead there was only a click.

Hank sighed in relief. At last, the detective was out of bullets.

"Plan B, then," Garton said. He gripped his gun by the barrel and pistol-whipped Hank across the face.

Hank flopped down like a rag-doll, and knew no more.

6.

In the Hollywood Room of Castle Kantlove, Dr. Kantlove and Lolita were celebrating their great success. All over the world, national leaders were pledging their countries' whole treasuries to him, if only he would stop the missile attacks. The mad couple were dancing with the stars—literally. The floor was made out of the same star tiles that were used on the Hollywood Walk of Fame. In the background, wax sculptures of James Mason, Malcolm McDowell, R. Lee Ermey, and many others leered at them. Dr. Kantlove had received these figures as payment from Madame Tussaud's in exchange for not blowing up all their museums.

Lolita sighed, and leaned her head on Kantlove's broad chest. "Oh, Werny, this is wonderful! It reminds me of our wedding day, when I became Frau Kantlove!"

Kantlove wasn't in quite the same romantic mood as his partner. As she stepped on her his foot for the thousandth time, he rolled his eyes and muttered, "More like Frau Kant*dance*."

"What was that?"

"Nothink, nothink, mein dear."

As he continued dancing, Kantlove wondered to himself, as he often did, why exactly he kept Lolita around. She was far from being his intellectual equal, obviously enough, and many of his more involved science experiments bored her. He knew that she had cheated on him several times, with the guards and with others, and yet he always forgave her. Maybe it was because he couldn't stand the thought of blowing something up with a missile without a sexy woman on his lap. True, he had been suffering from his curse for some time, but that had only deepened his need for the sublimation of eroticized explosions...and someone to share them with.

Lolita stepped away from him suddenly, interrupting his thoughts.

"Hey, this dancing's getting a little dull," she said. "How 'bout we blow something up?"

The doctor's face lit up with delight. "Why, you have just read mein mind, Liebling!" She really had—the merest thought of blowing things up with her had got his Jäegermeister flowing.

She scoffed. "I can't *read*, silly," she giggled.

He ignored her remark. He was figuring this was as good a time as any to tell her about what he'd been thinking about recently.

"I have reached an important decision, mein little schnitzel."

"What is it?"

"I have decided not to blow up any more historical monuments or buildings."

Lolita's excitement faded from her face. "What? Why?!"

"I'm going to up...ze ante!"

"I don't understand. You're doing what with your auntie?"

"Monuments and buildings are too *small* of kartoffels, darlink! No—*now* I am going to send a Saturn Five rocket into space, to blow up the moon!"

"You could really do that?" Lolita said, overjoyed again.

"It'll be a cakevalk!"

She waggled finger-guns at him. "Don't you mean...moonwalk?"

"Zoom, zoom—to der moon!" he exclaimed, with a laugh.

He took her hand, and the two of them walked to the control room. Lolita waved goodbye to the sculpture of James Dean as they left—Kantlove tried not to be jealous.

"Why are the guys always so stiff in there?" she asked. He didn't grace that question with a reply.

Soon they were back in the control room, where the rocket launch panel awaited them. Kantlove had already loaded the cockpit on the Saturn Five with a robot that would deploy a moon-destroying bomb. He just had to launch it.

"Are you ready, mein love?" he asked. He sat at the controls, and she sat on his lap again.

"I'm *always* ready...for you," she said sweetly.

Kantlove placed his finger over the button. "You know, I've alvays hated that dolt Ralph Kramden," he said, "from that abominable Amerikaner TV series, *Der Honeymooners*."

"Never seen it," Lolita said.

"I've alvays longed to strip Kramden's catchphrase of meaning. Now, at last, I vill!"

He pressed the launch button, and at once, the rocket zoomed up into the Earth's stratosphere. Unlike its predecessors, it escaped Earth's atmosphere and gravity, and passed into the starry void beyond.

"It vill need a secondary fueling-up to reach das moon," the mad scientist said. "I vill take manual control and guide it to the fuel satellite."

He plugged in the Xbox controller that allowed him to steer the rocket. Once it connected through the Bluetooth adapter, he turned the rocket on its side, and brought into a roughly geo-orbital course.

The fuel satellite was dead ahead, just where it was supposed to be. The satellite took the shape of a large, gaping ring of metal, into which the nosecone of the rocket would be inserted. An injector arm would extend and use vacuum-suction to implant the fuel into the rocket.

When the head of the missile synced up with the receptors,

however, something happened. Kantlove watched as the rocket was pushed backwards by the receiver arms, before being drawn back into the satellite again. Then the arms pushed it back out, only to draw it back in once more. This pump-action continued back and forth for a few awkward minutes.

"Aw, they're makin' a baby," Lolita said, tilting her head.

"Enough of this!" Kantlove cried. "Ve should have enough gas to make the moon without refueling."

He pulled the rocket away from the metal structure and turned it towards Earth's natural satellite. He poured on all the speed the ship could muster, and within a few minutes, the sensors detected the pull of the moon's gravity. Kantlove turned off the engines and pressed the button to launch the lander capsule. Both the rocket and the capsule drifted slowly down to the rocky-gray landscape.

Kantlove cackled, and waited for the robot to open the hatch of the lander. Once it stepped out onto the lunar surface, all it had to do was activate the bomb—and it was bye-bye, moon! No more tides, no more moonlit dates, no more werewolves. Time for a new era.

But instead of the robot, something else stepped out of the capsule. A small figure wearing a spacesuit.

Kantlove had many cameras on the moon, and using one of them he zoomed in on the small astronaut's visor. It was Leonard, his experimental test monkey—Kantlove had given him a semblance of intelligence with one of his serums. He still wasn't very bright, though. That dumb chimp had taken the bomb robot's place on the rocket! He always did write about wanting to go to the moon when he was placed at one of Kantlove's infinite typewriters.

"Vun of these days, Kramden," Kantlove bellowed. "Vun of these days!"

7.

When Hank once again returned to consciousness, he was in a jail cell. His ragged clothes had been taken away and replaced with a suit of prison orange. His hands were bound behind his back by handcuffs. He was alone. Alone, except for the shame and the guilt of what he had done.

Once he was awake, his mind was clearer than it had been since he had changed. His memories were restored to him, and he understood fully what he had done.

He had killed people. Crushed them. He had wreaked havoc across the city, started destroying cars and buildings and everything in between. He brought his city, his *home*, to ruin.

There was a mirror in the cell, a large one, and when he first spotted himself in it, he didn't see his normal face. Instead he saw the lumpy, hairless purple face of that *monster*. It seemed to smile mockingly at him, delighting in the chaos it had unleashed.

He knew then it was his work that had done this—the serum. His anger had gotten the better of him. He was so eager to finish the experiments and rub it in Darwin's face that he had gone and thrown his whole life away.

Because there was no life after this. He may have come up with the formula in a fit of passion but he knew the ins and outs of its composition. These effects were permanent. He would always carry this demon, this Bulk, within him.

But maybe he could still find a purpose. After all, someone had to make sure no one else found that formula.

This curse couldn't be passed onto anyone else.

And furthermore, no one of evil intent could ever be allowed to become a Bulk.

Just then, footsteps started coming down the hall. Hank couldn't see much from his cell, and so he gasped when Ray Garton strode into view.

Garton's eyes had dark bags under them, like he had been crying his eyes out. He probably had, because of what Hank— what the *Bulk*—had done to his partner.

Garton didn't say anything. He just stared into Hank's eyes. He wanted him to stew.

Eventually, Hank gave in, and spoke first. "Look," he said. "I'm sorry about what happened to your partner. It was an accident, I swear. I didn't mean to kill her or anyone else!"

Garton spat on the floor. "An accident?" he cried. "No, an accident is shitting yourself in your sleep. What you did is called murder. And the only just penalty in *my* personal courtroom? Is death."

"It *was* an accident. An experiment gone crazy."

Garton slammed his fist against the bars in anger, and tried to hide the pain this caused him. "I don't know what the fuck you are, you sick weirdo. But you're going to pay for what you've done. I'm gonna make sure you rot in Hell, freak!"

Once again, the gun was in his hand. And this time, he had reloaded.

"Wait, you can't do this!" Hank exclaimed. "*This* is murder! You can't kill me just because you're a cop!"

"What are you gonna do, tough guy?" Garton shrugged. "Clearly I caught you trying to escape..."

He squeezed the trigger, and Hank dropped to the ground. A single jerk of motion, and it was over. He was stone-cold dead.

"Damn, that was more satisfying than it ought've been," Garton said. "Hey, you need a Band-Aid in there?"

He laughed at his own joke.

"Oh, sorry, did you ask for something? I can't hear very well now."

He laughed again.

Something was wrong. Garton knew he was acting strangely. Even though he was a cop, he wasn't always this sadistic.

Something in the air was making him angry. Something that weighed on him even more than Lisa's death.

He just couldn't figure out what it was—

Clink-clink-clink.

A ringing sound echoed out from the cell. Garton had turned away from the corpse for a moment. He looked into the cell and tried to see if anything had changed, if the dead man had moved at all. *Something* had caused that noise.

That was when he caught a glimpse of something on the floor, sparkling in the light—a bullet.

The bullet he had fired into Hank's skull.

His tissues had rejected it. Flung it back out of the wound.

The limp body in the cell began to stir.

"Oh God!" Garton choked out. "Damn bastard's pulling a *Night of the Living Dead!*" Then he coughed. The air was starting to turn red around him, and things were getting blurry.

Hank Howard slowly sat back up. He had a small flesh-wound in his forehead, where the bullet had struck. It was bleeding purple.

Before Hank knew it, that strange storm churned up inside him again. He was swallowed up by a rush of crackling winds, which howled deafeningly within the confines of the cell.

When the winds passed, his muscles had once again swollen up, and his skin had taken on that by-now familiar purple hue. The Amazing Bulk, back again, let out a monstrous roar.

Garton hadn't counted on this. He had no idea that his hasty act would unleash the devil again…

"Stay back! Stay back!"

He thought he had killed him. But he hadn't *wanted* to kill him. Not really. Garton knew he could be tough sometimes but he didn't murder suspects—Hank was innocent until proven guilty.

No...it had something to do with...with something in the room. Maybe that red gas that was covering everything.

Red gas...?

"Oh my God, the room's full of gas!" the detective said suddenly. "I-I feel funny, I..."

And then the bald man fell over and passed out.

Hank could feel himself within the Bulk, watching helplessly through his eyes. He could feel anger surging through him, but—

But this anger wasn't coming from him. It *was*, but it was unnatural somehow.

The Bulk, which seemed suddenly like a separate entity within himself, was succumbing to the rage that this crimson gas seemed to induce. He was getting angrier and angrier, and gaining size with that anger—he was swelling up inside the cell, pressing tight against the walls.

Hank knew this gas. It was one of his failed experiments, a product of his efforts to create the General's formula. It had made Billy 64 and 65 freak out and kill each other. But how had someone gotten their hands on that—?

One of the Bulk's rapidly-growing hands lashed out towards the cell mirror. It shattered to pieces, and at once, he saw that it was one of those one-way interrogation mirrors. He was being watched this whole time: the sight of a man in grand military uniform, wearing a gas mask, seemed to answer all his questions.

It was General Darwin.

"Makes you mad, doesn't it, dirtbag?" Darwin barked. His voice was muffled through his mask. "Rage is the spirit of war, son. Give into it."

The Bulk was wavering. The anger was so great that it was wearing on his central nervous system. Fatigue and a feverish sickness was coming over him. He struggled to calm down, but he was *so angry*…

The purple giant staggered and fell forward. His heavy weighed made him plow straight through the prison bars. He shuddered, and then, still unconscious, he shrank back into Hank Howard.

And the rage-red gas, the very breath of the war-god Mars, danced around the only man still standing, the man who considered himself the very avatar of combat.

* * *

Hank was getting really goddamn tired of passing out and waking up again. This was, like, the fourth time today he'd woken up somewhere different from where he passed out.

Once again, memories streamed back to him—it felt like a nightmare. Perhaps it had been a nightmare. Garton had tried to kill him—and Darwin had been watching, the whole time. He had set all of this up. And he used the failed formula—R9-14, he thought it was—to drive the Bulk crazy with rage, until…well, apparently until his body gave out, like people fainting from a panic attack.

Hank was losing his sense of what was real in his life, and what wasn't. How fitting, then, that he had traded his shredded prison outfit for a straitjacket. He was locked up in a padded cell, which had a glass observation window at the far end.

He breathed slowly, trying to steady himself. Suddenly, he realized he was very, very scared.

That fear only deepened when General Darwin, now sans gas mask, stepped into view in the observation window.

"What's up, doc?" he asked, with another of his cruel chuckles.

"You did this to me, Darwin!" Hank shouted. "The serum! It made me into a monster!"

Darwin's smile faded, but his arrogant sense of triumph

lingered. "Affirmative!" he said. "You finally achieved the results we were looking for!"

Hank stared at him in shock. He'd heard of crappy in-laws before, but this took the goddamn cake.

"Are you nuts? I just wrecked half, or, like, a decent quarter of the city, I—" He caught himself. "I killed innocent people. *That's* the result you wanted?"

"You shouldn't tire yourself out on questions, son. You're about to undergo an intense evaluation. We need to learn everything we can about your...condition."

"What, to cure me? Or use me as a guinea pig?" Hank snorted. "You might as well give me a lobotomy."

"Negative—that would be a waste of a great genius." Darwin laughed. "Let's talk about something more important."

"Like what?"

Darwin folded his arms in front of his chest. "You've given us the serum that will allow us to enhance a human—to make him more than human. Superhuman! You ought to be congratulated."

"What, for giving the military the power to kill even more people? Aren't drones enough?" Hank shook his head in disgust. "If you're here to give me an award, do me a favor and shove it up your ass."

Darwin clicked his tongue. "Look, no one was expecting you to inject yourself with the serum. That was truly idiotic of you."

"I agree," Hank replied. "Yeah, as much as I hate to agree with you on anything, I agree with you on that. But I did it for Hannah. I wanted to be a success for you, and have your blessing to marry her."

"I understand," Darwin said, "and that's why I give you permission to have my daughter's hand in marriage."

Hank's eyes widened in shock. But he quickly lapsed back into depression.

"It's too late—I'm a monster. I can't conform to society. I know what triggers the beast inside me: rage. But you know that all too well."

Darwin nodded.

"It's true—rage is what sets it off. But there's hope. Our boys have already analyzed your serum, and we're pretty sure we can formulate a cure."

"Then where is it?" Hank demanded. "Give it to me already! Why am I still imprisoned?"

Darwin cleared his throat.

"I was getting to that. Before we administer any sort of antidote, there's something you must do for us. Rather, for your country—your Uncle Sam."

Hank raised an eyebrow. "What are you driving at? I knew there'd be a catch with a goddamned tyrant like you."

"You're the only hope mankind has to surviving," Darwin said, ignoring the insult. "So it'd be wise for you to get serious."

"You sound sincere—like you really mean it. But honesty just ain't your strong suit, Jonathan." The General bristled wordlessly at a civilian using his first name. "But y'know," Hank went on, "I'm a nice guy. I'll hear you out."

Darwin sighed, and said, "There is a madman by the name of Dr. Kantlove. We don't know much about him, though we suspect that he may be a relative of a former scientific advisor to the President."

"Go on," Hank said.

"He's been sending off rockets, blowing up monuments around the world. The chaos started around the same time that you developed the serum. I'm afraid much of the world has been gripped by mass hysteria…which is too bad. I'd hoped I could expect my fellow countrymen to be less pussy-ish in the face of adversity…"

"Well, how do I fit into all this?"

"I was getting to that. We need to turn superhuman and destroy him." When Hank didn't respond, the General added: "You haven't forgotten how much destruction you're capable of causing, have you, Howard?"

"Of course not. How could I ever?"

"We know where his base is, but his defenses there are too strong. So we're going to drop you in at a distance, and you'll go run in and eliminate him."

"I can't take another human life," Hank said, shaking his head. "Especially not on some...shadow mission for the U.S. military."

"So you can kill innocent people, but you can't kill the enemy? What kind of monster are you anyway?"

"*I didn't kill anyone!* It was that thing, that—that Bulk!"

Hank's rage rippled through him, and though his muscles didn't grow, he could feel his skin turn purple. His veins bulged in his forehead as his face became the portrait of fury.

But then he saw another figure standing in the window. A woman.

Hannah.

She was frightened of him.

"Hannah!" he cried. "Hannah!"

A soldier appeared, and ushered Hannah away. She clearly struggled against the escort, but she was still clearly terrified.

Darwin pressed on, lacking pity in every cell of his body.

"So do you accept the mission?" he asked. "Do you accept your fate? Are you ready to save the world?"

"Yes!" Hank shouted. Then, he sank back into himself. His skin regained its normal shade.

He shook his head again and said, "Y'know, screw the world. I'm doing this for two people: me and Hannah. I promise you, I will make the world safe for her and I. We *will* be together. And if that means becoming that hideous beast once more—so be it."

The General grinned broadly.

"Good," he said. "Here's the game plan..."

8.

Aboard the military drop-jet, Hank was whistling a song that was stuck in his head. The pilot could hear the tune, and he was starting to get irritated. He had a feeling he was being mocked.

At last, he snapped. "How *dare* you make fun of 'When Johnny Comes Marching Home!'"

Hank stopped whistling and looked up.

"I wasn't making fun of anything."

"Yes, you were! You think it's funny to whistle patriotic wartime songs around an Air Force pilot? I bet you think the military is a big waste of money, don't you?"

"No comment," Hank said, rolling his eyes. "*I* always thought the song I was whistling was about ants."

The pilot grumbled quietly to himself. "I tell ya," he said, lifting a hand off the controls to tug at his collar, "I get no respect."

Hank was dissuaded from whistling. The two sat in silence for the next few dozen miles.

At last, the pilot cleared his throat and started talking again. "Alright, we're coming up to the checkpoint," he said. "Any closer and Kantlove will spot us on his radar. You ready?"

Hank patted the parachute on his back. "All set."

The pilot nodded.

"Come marching home, Johnny," he said.

Hank nodded, not knowing what else to make of the words.

The back of the plane dropped open, and suddenly Hank was standing over the rushing tan canvas of the desert. He hesitated a moment, and then took the plunge.

The air screamed around him as he fell—its icy talons tore at his skin. He tugged hard on the parachute ripcord, and felt a jerk in his shoulders as the fabric hoisted him up. Then he descended slowly onto the desert's coarse sands.

Through the shimmering air, Hank could see Kantlove's castle looming in the distance. The sight of it filled him with dread.

But the Bulk would feel no such dread. There wasn't anything that monster was afraid of.

"Okay," Hank sighed, "time to get angry."

He tried to think of what his body felt like when he was angry. He clenched every muscle in his body tightly and made an angry face.

All that did was make him snicker to himself. And laughter was *not* going to turn him into the Bulk.

"This is no time for clowning around. Time to break out the secret weapon."

Hank reached into his pocket, and fished out a picture of General Darwin. He had specifically requested a picture of the General making his smuggest, shit-eatingest grin, and the base personnel had delivered.

His arrogance filled Hank's heart with *hate!*

Hank began to tremble; the terrible storm that signaled the coming of the Bulk was rumbling inside him once more.

The desert air swelled with the sound of rushing gales and thunderbolts, and soon, the elephantine feet of the Amazing Bulk were pounding the hot sand.

The Bulk saw the castle, as Hank had, and knew what he had to do.

With a raging war-cry, he took off at top speed towards the

towering structure. The roar could be heard from the castle's high turrets, which happened to be manned at this time of day by small cadres of Kantlove's Roman-dressed guards.

"Did you hear that?" whispered one of the guards, who was named Spartacus. "It—it sounded like a monster!"

"Where the hell did it come from?" the other one, Crassus, asked.

They stared out into the desert. Off in the distance, they could see a purple shape rushing towards them. "Purple...?" one of them whispered.

What sort of animal could move that fast that was *purple*?

Once it got within a certain range, they could see it wasn't an animal. It was—it was a *dude*.

A big, purple, bald, angry dude, who was staring straight at them with his gross, fucked-up eyes.

"Oh shit!" Crassus yelled. "Open fire!"

They took out their assault rifles and let the monster have it.

But their fates were already sealed. The Bulk was coming up to a large boulder which was nestled in the sand. With a single kick from his strong foot, he launched the big rock like a missile straight towards the turret.

"*Aaaaaaghhhh—!!*"

Spartacus and Crassus screamed and died together, pulped by the onrushing stone.

Between the two of them, though, they had killed around thirty or forty innocent people during their time working for Kantlove, so it was decently okay that they died.

Now all the guards were watching the Bulk as he continued his approach. He had sacrificed a little momentum in kicking the boulder, but he was swiftly gaining back the speed he'd lost. Upon reaching the outer walls of Kantlove's fortress he used his velocity to drive his hands deep into the stone bricks. Then, summoning all of his strength, he scaled the wall, yard by yard, until he had crossed over into the inner courtyards. His roars and thundering footsteps shook the castle down to its roots. The guards immediately sprang into action—they had a job to do.

Dr. Kantlove was sitting in the castle's control room, plotting his next strike on the moon, when he heard the rumbling reverberations. Stanley the dog sat on his lap.

"Vhat in the name of science?!" the doctor exclaimed. Stanley looked up in surprise and yelped.

Replacing the sound of shaking stone was another noise, one the doctor strained to make out. It was an awful noise, and as time passed, it slowly became more and more clear. Suddenly, both dog and doctor started trembling—for they realized what they were hearing was a chorus of screams. And with it, another horrific sound: the unmistakable noise of limb being torn from limb.

At once, the shaking, sweating mad doctor turned towards the control panel for the local surveillance systems. He swatted at the buttons until he found a camera that showed him what was going on.

His horror only deepened when he saw the monster for himself. A super-strong purple titan who jiggled like gelatin—he never suspected such things could be. And it was killing his men, swatting them down one by one as though they were only insects.

Kantlove gulped. "Nein—das ist nicht gut..." he said softly, shaking his head. This was a red alert situation—he had to figure out what to do.

"Vhere are mein personal guards?" he cried out. Then he caught himself. "Oh, ja, that's right...I had them all killed."

The outer guards, the pawns, they had always been around solely for the purpose of sacrifice. And they were performing that role to a T. Their bullets were as nothing next to this mysterious monster, who was making an absolute mess of the Kantlove ancestral home with the blood of the slaughtered legionnaires.

A few of the guards were able to dodge the Bulk's sweeping attacks, but he was driving them deeper into the castle, down into the dungeons. As he pushed them back towards the open stairs to the castle's under-levels, the Bulk accidentally triggered a tripwire which spanned across the hallway. A giant round boulder, much like the one he'd kicked at the turret, broke loose from a secret chamber above the staircase entry, and started bounding down the steps. The retreating guards had nowhere to go but down. They ran from the huge rock as fast as they could, but the stone only gained speed the farther it fell. Save for one, all of them were crushed until its merciless weight. The sole survivor among them had been a track star back in high school, and his feets weren't failing him now. The Bulk, seeking his blood, followed him and the boulder down the stairs.

Kantlove watched on the monitor as the fleeing guard passed by the various torture devices that filled the dank, slimy underground chamber. The iron maiden, the stretching rack, the pit and the pendulum, the headphones which constantly played Ted Nugent songs—all of these and more had reduced the doctor's many enemies to tears and pleas for mercy over the years. All of these victims, once they had been wrung clean of information, had been thrown down into the abyss that yawned open below the castle.

A thin bridge crossed over this abyss, which Kantlove's men called the Bridge of Bhazad-boom. It was slippery and hard to run on, and if one stayed standing on it too long, the chatter of the goblin-men Kantlove had engineered and discarded could be heard echoing up from the depths. But the guard knew that if he reached this bridge, he'd be safe. He ran to the center of it, and then, after finding his balance, he stopped.

The boulder kept coming at him, but it wobbled once it rolled onto the Bridge. The guard stayed steady, staring forward hopefully. The boulder wobbled more and more precariously before it slipped off of the rail-thin Bridge into the darkness below.

The guard didn't have time to relax—because now the Bulk was upon him. And despite his seeming clumsiness, the Bulk could traverse the Bridge of Bhazad-Boom without losing his balance. He chased the guard across the Bridge to where another segment of the torture chamber could be found. The narrow doorway that led into this part of the dungeon was sealed shut with a locked metal hatch. Now the Bulk had the man cornered.

The guard's face was an expression of pure horror. His hands pressed against the door's cold, moist steel, but there was no escape now. The Bulk was thundering towards him, roaring like a hellish demon.

"*Nooooo!!!!*" screamed the guard, raising his hands in front of his face. "*Noooooo!!!!!*"

The Bulk loomed over him, menacingly. The guard shook his head, as if trying to wake up from a nightmare.

"*Noooooo!!!! NOOOOOOO!!!!*"

The Bulk stared at him with his rheumy white eyes.

"*NOOOOO!!!!!NOOOOOO-HOHOHOHOHOH—OOOOO!! NOOOOOOOOOOOOOOOOOOOOOOOOOOO!!!!!!*"

The Bulk raised his giant foot and squished the man flat as a pancake.

Kantlove was horrified; he tried to think quickly. His secret assassin and head of security, Alexis, was out on PTO. His deadly plague-agent, the disease that walked, wasn't yet combat-ready. He could activate the subterranean supercomputer, let *her* take over, but even he feared what that mechanical madwoman could do.

There was no other choice, then—he had to flee! There was an escape pod in the control room, but it was for Stanley. The little dog was frequently a thorn in Kantlove's side but he did love him. In the event of an emergency, the order of evacuation went Stanley, Kantlove, the money, the research papers, Lolita, and finally, the guards. He placed Stanley in the pod and closed the seal-hatch; then, he pressed the button which ignited the micro-rocket on the pod's underside. With a yipe of surprise, Stanley flew off into the wild blue yonder, where he would land somewhere safe.

With Stanley taken care of, Kantlove turned towards the next most important person: himself. The castle was shaking even harder now—that creature was getting closer.

"This is even worse than that time that flying saucer broke down and that little gray alien came to the door to use the phone," Kantlove gasped.

There was nothing left to do. He found the nearest exit and started booking it to his escape craft.

The doctor was not a young man anymore—his knees were going stiff on him. He ran with the gait of a drunken penguin, and his tongue panted in and out of his mouth like a dog's. His lips were dry, and he licked them incessantly. His cane thumped heavily across the floor with each lurching step.

"Mama Kantlove alvays said my temper vould be the death of me," he moaned. "I believe the last time she said it vas on the phone right before I had a missile sent to her for Mother's Day."

He had made his way down into the castle's shipping bay, a large warehouse space stacked high with crates containing munitions and other valuables. If he could make it to the far end he'd be in the main hangar—his escape ship was there. Just a few more yards, and he'd be home free...

Kantlove froze in his tracks when he saw the crates ahead of him began to move. A great tower of them fell forward, having been pushed over with terrible force. With a heavy slam the crates blocked his path. The shambling form of the Amazing Bulk stepped out into his path, and let out a horrible roar.

"Vhat do you vant from me?!" Kantlove screamed, as he pissed himself.

The Bulk only let out another cry of rage.

"Please, spare my life!" the doctor howled. "I am a scientist! I am Dr. Werner von Can't-Love...I mean, Kantlove! Vhat is it, a girl you vant? Maybe I can help...you know Frankenstein? Who do you think it vas who set him up with his Bride, eh?"

The Bulk *did* want a girl, a very specific one, but he wasn't going to tell Kantlove that. Instead, he swung his titanic fist straight at the doctor's ribcage.

The punch hit Kantlove so hard that his heart burst out of his back—it flew across the warehouse before smacking down on the floor with a wet plop. He'd been called heartless before, but this was ridiculous.

"Oh, scheisse," Kantlove said. Kant*live* would be a more appropriate name now. "Auf wiedersehn, cruel world!"

He fell hard to the ground, and it was done—Dr. Kantlove was dead.

* * *

Lolita had felt the shaking and heard the screams, but figured that was probably normal. She was putting her mind to work on multitasking—namely, walking and chewing gum at the same time. It wasn't particularly easy for her.

As she crossed into the shipping bay, in search of Dr. Kantlove, she blew a pink bubble from her gum. She was surprised by how big she was able to make it—then, it popped in her face. The pink rubbery substance coated her face and sealed her eyes shut.

"Hey! Who turned out the lights?"

She tried for a moment or two to peel it off, only to determine it was impossible. She could see a little bit through the gum, so she tried to wander forward.

"Hey, bumblebee, are you down here? Can you help me?" Lolita's voice shook. "I think I've gone blind!"

She could see a large shape ahead of her, roughly man-sized. She approached it.

"Pookie bear? Is that you—oh!"

She bumped against the great mass, and heard someone groan.

"Baby?" She reached out with her hand, and found herself touching an expanse of flesh. It was smooth, but hard, rigid with muscle. She giggled flirtatiously.

"So *that's* where you've been spending your free time—at the gym!" She felt the sleek, toned muscles. "I think Baby likes this," she cooed sexily.

She reached down, and *another* expanse of flesh met her hand.

"Oh, baby! My, how you've grown since we last played!"

She reached up to try to peel away the gum once more. "I gotta see this! This is historic!"

The gum had dried a little, so it was a little easier to peel a layer of it off. Now she could see her Werny Wern for herself…

Only it wasn't Werner. It was his killer—the Bulk.

Lolita didn't really comprehend. She stuffed the gum back into her mouth, and said through it, "'Aby, wha' happa' 'oo 'er *face*? I 'ov i'!"

She blew another bubble right as the Bulk's fist flew towards her. The bubble popped—and then, in a messier fashion, so did her head. It was over so quick that a brain like hers didn't have time to register pain.

* * *

The Bulk's mission was complete, and so the storm came again to replace him with Hank. Hank looked grimly at Lolita Schiller's gory remains, and he knelt down towards her hand. She was wearing the ring—*his* ring, the ring he was going to give Hannah. He had finally reclaimed it, after Scully had taken it from him.

Hank retrieved his radio from where he'd stored it, and he tuned to the frequency that Darwin had directed him to use.

"General, are you there?"

After a moment, there was a crackle, and then:

"Copy, Howard, I read you, over."

"I've eliminated Dr. Kantlove," and here Hank pronounced the first syllable of Kantlove wrong, though not in the way most people did it, "along with all of his gang. I'm ready to be picked up now, over."

Silence.

Hank frowned. Something was wrong.

Wasn't this it? Wasn't this supposed to be the end of the mission—?

Suddenly, the castle shook, and the sound of an explosion could be heard.

Hank looked up, and saw in horror that the brickwork of the ceiling was splitting open. The ceiling was coming down on him!

One of the shipping containers he'd knocked over as the Bulk had broken open. A few of Kantlove's smuggled trinkets had been stored in this crate, stuff like the Ark of the Covenant, the Holy Grail, Excalibur, rubbish like that. Hank climbed over the scattered plunder and hid inside the container. He covered his eyes and ears as the falling ceiling smashed down on the metal crate's roof; dust swept in, covering Hank and making him cough.

Once a second or two passed he pulled up the RADIO again.

"Excuse me—what the fuck was that?! Over!"

He dashed out of the crate and looked up into where the ceiling had once been. Just then, two fighter jets passed over, letting loose a rocket payload.

"Holy shit!" Hank shouted. He ran into the depths of the warehouse, hoping the evade the missiles. The explosion was deafening, and knocked him to the ground, but he was unhurt.

Once again, he shouted into the radio. "Air Force jets are attacking me, General!" he cried. "Something's wrong, they must think I'm the enemy! Call them off!"

Hank's heart dropped when he heard the General sigh. He knew then that he'd been tricked.

"I'm afraid I haven't been telling the truth, Hank."

"I should've fucking known."

"There is no antidote. No cure. You can never return to your normal self. You see, Hank, funding for the project ended two years ago. The government lost interest—the window for results was even narrower than I ever let you know. So I had to look elsewhere for funding. Dr. Kantlove was more than willing to dole out the required cash. He was hoping to use the super-soldier formula to fix his legendary impotence, for which the world had always mocked him.

"Now that you've successfully achieved a working formula, I no longer needed Kantlove's backing. So I had to take care of him, or rather, have you take care of him. Once I tell the President that I led the operation that terminated such an infamous terrorist, on top of providing him with an army of invincible, Bulky soldiers, I'll be up to my neck in medals!"

"You're crazy," Hank said. "You're sick!"

"Your opinion doesn't matter now, son," the General replied. "Now I must eliminate you, too."

"You fucking bastard!"

But it was no use—Darwin had cut off the call.

And the jets were swooping back again—he could hear their machine guns chatter.

There was only one thing that could save him. He had to give into his rage once again.

Hank had lost track of how many times he'd changed. But that didn't matter now. All that mattered was that he was the Bulk again—and he was running. He was running as fast as he could.

Once the Bulk got within a certain distance of the warehouse wall, and made a flying leap towards it. He smashed straight through the bricks and came out into the castle courtyard. But he didn't slow down for a second—he plowed through the outer wall as well. Now he was back out in the sunny desert, and he kept on running.

Two jets at his back—guns spewing streams of bullets—and dozens of miles separating him from any sort of cover.

It was take every ounce of his speed to survive this encounter.

Hannah's voice echoed in his mind: *Run, Hank! Run!*

9.

Far above the desert where the jets were chasing down the Bulk, beyond the clouds, an alien spacecraft was hovering.

"I say, chaps," said Theodore, the first officer of the flying saucer, "that Bulk fellow seems to be having a rough time of it down there, wot?"

Theodore's fellow gray aliens nodded. "It's really quite a spot of bother for him, I'm afraid," Edward the captain affirmed.

Edward and Theodore were joined on the bridge of their flying saucer by Clarence, the engineer. All of them were enjoying their cups of gronumulum tea, which was their customary beverage for watching the monitor with.

They had come to this silly little planet, this "Irth," in hopes of finding some amusement. They had been watching Hank's journey from the very beginning, or at least, since he had gone to go pick up Hannah to take her to the carnival. They had become quite invested, as human beings do with soap operas or reality shows.

Like any fans of any given entertainment medium, they had started discussing their takes on what they were watching.

"You know, chums, I have to feel like our interest in this Bulk has to have another dimension to it," said Clarence, tapping out his pipe. "There's some sort of intellectual element to these proceedings, wouldn't you say? Even if it's merely an *emergent* quality, there's just a resonance to these events, yes?"

"I certainly agree," Edward affirmed. "I mean, the mythology of this 'Irth' seems veritably haunted by stories about these kinds of dualistic shapeshifters. There was that Stevenson fellow, he wrote about a scientist turning into a monster against his will."

"Yes, uh, Dogdoor Dzichul ond Meesster Heed, I think they called it," said Theodore. "Barbarous tongue, this Irth dialect. Anyway, in that story, a man drinks a potion and turns into a brute who terrorizes his home city. It's a whole allegory about the struggle between good and evil."

Edward chuckled. "Good and evil, my goodness! They've lofty ideals, these humans. What a silly binary to waste time debating over. Clearly evil is always the correct answer."

"Indubitably," nodded Clarence. "But I don't think that the Bulk is an evil counterpoint to the goodness in Hank."

"No, not at all," the captain agreed. "Instead, I think we must look at Stevenson's inspiration: the werewolf stories of the medieval period. Those stories fundamentally represent the struggle between beast and man—a dichotomy which emerges from humanity's own recognition of the process of evolution, wherein self-aware humans arose from intrinsically unaware animal forms."

"Yes, if the Bulk is a werewolf, then he represents humanity's fear of atavism, the resurgence of primeval traits," Theodore said. "That, in turn, implies that a narrative of forward progress is essential to the human mind. People seeks to move on from the past into the future because they understand that the future's innovations will improve their lives and those of their offspring. That's something that a werewolf, a beast-man, ultimately stands against. He threatens to drag humanity back into their animal ancestry" He laughed at his own cleverness, and rubbed the top of his hairless, big-eyed gray head with his long, flaccid fingers. "This is reflected in how Hank seeks to build a family life with

Hannah—by having children with her, which is the fundamental purpose of the marriage rite, he is fulfilling his nature-given role of perpetuating the future of his species. The evolutionary forces that guide him give him this fear of his Bulkish self."

"This drive to perpetuate the family also ties in with his fear of becoming a social pariah: the natural desire to reproduce also codifies the norms of human society, as humans must protect each other in order to protect the reproductive cycle," said Clarence. "Being an exile significantly harms one's chances of contributing to the gene pool, which runs against the purpose of being alive. This induces a desire for conformity—as represented symbolically by the character of General Darwin."

"So, we're in agreement, then?" Edward asked. "The story surrounding Hank Howard and the Amazing Bulk is about how mortal beings are prisoners of their own instincts, specifically the biological drive to reproduce, and the tragedy of that condition's negative influence upon the complex emotional self?"

"I'd like to play devil's advocate, if I may," Theodore put it. "Consider the possibility that this ontological and teleological analysis of the Bulk is inadequate. Maybe his identity makes more sense under the lens of, say, a feminist or Marxist critique."

"Oh, really, Teddy, that's too much," declared Clarence, half-seriously.

"Well, it's not an uncommon interpretation of Stevenson's novel that the brute character the scientist turns into is symbolism for the perceived corruptive influence of class sympathy, or even the homosexuality of the protagonist."

"So you think that Hank is a middle-class lad who turns into a brutish working-class man when he gets angry?" The engineer snorted. "Can't say it sounds terribly likely. In fact, it sounds somewhat offensive, if one does truly have sympathy for the working class."

"The gay postulation might make a little bit of sense," Edward said, "given that lavender, or purple, is often symbolic of the queer community."

"And it would make sense that Hank would be afraid of something that's turning him away from his heterosexual bond with Hannah," Theodore added.

"But you can't reconcile the two theories," Clarence said. "If you presume the Bulk to be a representation of the fear of atavism, as well as a sort of gay panic scenario, then you're slandering gay people by default. Associating them with the primitive." He stroked the part of his face that ought to have been a chin. "Yet at the same time, I suppose we did draw the conclusion that a fear of atavism in some ways justifies the progressive impulse. That is to say, progressive thought satisfies a feeling of safety in the human mind via the belief that building towards the future is building away from the past."

"It's accepting fresh possibility over what's already historically happened," Edward concluded. "I guess the story of the Bulk has a lot to teach all of us. Though, I have to admit, I will probably forget everything we've talked about by the dawn of the next day-cycle."

"Me too," Theodore said. "Honestly, I think that the Bulk is actually just a parody-slash-mockbuster of various superhero conventions."

"Is there any more gronumulum tea, or whatever the bloody hell it's called?" Clarence asked.

The tea kettle was still on the stove, and they'd forgotten to turn the burner off. The stove was right next to the main fusion reactors. And so when the heat built up too much, the reactors overheated. A temperature cascade quickly flooded the combustion chambers, and so those oh-so volatile reactors exploded.

The ship was vaporized in orbit. The whole crew, including the trio on the bridge, were killed instantly. But there was a common phrase among their people, which they'd stolen from other aliens: "So it goes." And so it went.

10.

The Bulk had run many miles away from Castle Kantlove while the aliens were debating him. Once, he had glanced back, and saw that many jets were swarming over the castle, blowing it to bits with their missiles. They were trying to bury any evidence that connected Kantlove to General Darwin.

He was no different from that castle to these pilots—he was just evidence. But at least he was *fast* evidence. He was always a good stride ahead of the jets that were spraying bullets down on him.

But his little jog was soon going to come to an end. He crossed an admirable distance, but he couldn't go on forever.

Back in the control room, Darwin was getting impatient. The live feed from the jets was showing the futility of chasing the Bulk around the desert. He had hoped to avoid this, as he was sure that it would be difficult to answer for when he had that talk with the President. But he had no choice.

Duty wasn't a thing that made sense all the time, Darwin rationalized. Sometimes you had to do what seemed crazy at the time in order for good sense to have a chance later.

"Alright boys," he told the men at the control panel. "Drop the bomb."

"Yessir."

The transmission went out. One of the pilots in one of the jets received the signal.

"Copy that, control," he said. He sent the warning signal to his fellow pilot. The second jet swooped away, leaving only the one.

The pilot pressed a button, and the bottom flaps of the jet's bomb bay opened.

He would only have a few seconds in which to get away. This payload was a real whopper—this nuclear-charged baby was worth about fifteen hundred billion quazillion sticks of dynamite. Or something like that. The pilot had a tendency towards hyperbole when talking about the bomb, as he thought it was really awesome—the bomb, as it were.

You could blow up so much shit with this baby!

"Dropping disposal unit in 3...2..." He was sweating with pleasurable anticipation. "...1! Bombs away!"

He pressed the release trigger.

The bomb did not drop.

"Oh, shit, is it stuck?"

He looked back into the bomb chamber. Sure enough, the claw-arms that were gripping the bomb were locked in place.

The pilot sighed, and switched the controls over to autopilot. He silently cursed the Bulk, who made for a good scapegoat. As the plane coasted on, he climbed back into the bomb bay and started pushing down on the bomb.

He really should've known where this was going, especially when he climbed up on top of the bomb like it was a horse. This sort of thing had happened before in history. But the pilot had no reverence for history. His fingers pulled and pried at the claws, trying to force them open.

"Come on...come on!" he growled. "I just want to *kill!!*"

If only he'd been careful what he wished for.

The bomb broke loose of its restraints before the pilot had a chance to climb off. As he started to fall, he wondered if perhaps he hadn't chosen this for himself, of his own free will.

Maybe he had always wanted to blow himself up with one of the weapons which he so deeply loved.

Yeah...this wasn't so bad a fate, plummeting from the sky on the back of an atom bomb. This was for duty, after all, for king and country! He had no idea why Americans said that, as they had fought a war to get rid of kings, but he was proud to serve all the same. He let out a joyous victory cry as dropped down onto the Amazing Bulk.

The Bulk was starting to tire, after such a long chase. He could hear the whistle of the bomb dropping from the sky, and he looked up to see what it was.

Then everything turned white...and got really, really hot.

General Darwin was still watching it all on the video screen. His face relaxed for the first time in a long while. It was over. He'd won.

The second pilot, who'd saw his comrade fall to his doom, reported back in a shaky voice: "M-mission accomplished, sir."

"Good work, gentlemen," Darwin said. He didn't care that he was only addressing one gentleman. He let out a hearty sigh.

Then he turned around. And he saw the broken face of his daughter.

"Cupcake, what's wrong?" the General cooed. "How did you get in here?"

"What—what just happened?" Hannah asked. "Was that a nuclear explosion? Did—did something happen to Hank?"

Darwin took a moment to answer.

"Honey..." he said slowly, "Hank knew he was risking his life when he accepted this mission. He stopped Dr. Kantlove...he saved the world...but I'm afraid he got himself killed in the process. He was a very brave man. Never forget that."

Hannah's eyes seemed to swell under the magnification of her tears. She sank to her knees sobbing, and her father stepped up to her and patted her shoulder.

"I'm so sorry, dear," said the General, straining suddenly to repress a smile. "I'm so sorry."

Hannah cried a while longer, and then she asked to be taken home. The General went with her—he had no more business here.

As he followed her out of the control room, he looked back at the monitor screen. As the surviving pilot jetted away from the scene of the crime, he left behind a tremendous mushroom cloud —an image that could turn even the bravest person's blood cold. Even Darwin shuddered to consider the power that was at mankind's disposal.

But at least that power belonged to America. Other countries had it too, but they didn't have the army of Bulks, such as the one he was about to create.

Soon, America's day would come again, and the world would respect the Stars and Stripes, as they had before. And when America was great again, Darwin could at last die a happy man.

* * *

For Hannah, the drive from the Army base back to the mansion was like a long nightmare. It rained on the way back and the images she saw through the car windows were smudged and distorted. It was like the whole world was being washed away from her. Now that Hank was gone, there was nothing holding things together in her life. The world was as cold and empty as a barren refrigerator.

When she got back to her room, and her father finally left her, she sat next to the window and cried for another hour or so. It was the sort of numb crying that doesn't have a bottom, that could go on and on for lifetimes. Eventually though it did stop, and Hannah, face red from tears, climbed into bed and went to sleep.

An hour passed...maybe two. The moon stared down on her with an apathetic gaze. Silence reigned over the house of the victorious General.

Then, Hannah woke up. She'd heard something smack against her window.

It must've just been a tree branch or something. She went back to sleep.

But the sound came again—a faint rap, like a pebble being thrown against glass.

She was sure she was just imagining it, but she had to go check. She rose from the bed and went to the window.

To her shock, there was a figure standing outside her window. And not just any figure: it was Hank. He'd climbed up onto the balcony that stood just outside her room.

"Hank!" she cried. "You're ali—"

"Shh!" he urged her. "Let me in, but quietly."

She opened the window, and he climbed inside. They sat together for a moment on the bed, staring in disbelief. Then, they embraced each other, and kissed.

"How—how did you—" she started to say, but he shushed her again.

"Don't worry about that now," he said. "Hannah, there's a question I've wanted to ask you for a very long time."

He produced the diamond ring, which he had taken from Lolita's body.

"Hannah...will you marry me?"

Her face suddenly seemed to glow.

"Yes!" she whisper-shouted. "Yes, of course!" She laughed. "Oh, this is amazing. You're alive! I have to tell Dad, and—"

"No!" Hank cautioned her. "Your father can't find me here. He tried to kill me with that A-bomb blast."

Her eyes darkened. "What? What do you mean? I can't believe that!"

"He thinks he succeeded, Hannah. He thinks he killed me."

"It—it can't be. Dad—wouldn't try to kill anyone. He—"

"I'm sorry, baby," Hank said sadly, "but it's the truth."

She could see from the look on his face that he had no reason to lie.

Just then, the door to her room was kicked in, and the lights snapped on. General Darwin stood in the doorway. When he saw Hank in the light, it looked like steam was going to come out of his ears.

"You bastard! You're supposed to be dead!"

Hank rose from the bed's edge and raised his hands, hoping he could have a chance to talk the old man down. But before he could prepare himself, the General charged towards him and threw his full weight into Hank's body. The enraged military officer thrust his hands around Hank's throat, choking him tightly.

"I'm gonna kill you once and for all, freak!" Darwin screamed.

"Not if I have anything to say about it, you...you dollar-store dictator!" Hank growled back.

The two of them struggled against each other, like wrestlers locked in the heat of a match. Hannah tried to separate them, to no avail. Hank was starting to turn purple, and as he did so his strength became irresistible.

But even though it had been quite some kind since General Darwin had fought another combatant mano-a-mano, he was immensely strong for a man of his age. He could hold Hank for now, even as some of the Bulk came into him.

"You really shoulda made that antidote!" Hank spat. The fear that was overtaking Darwin's face—the first true fear the man had shown in years—showed that the General shared Hank's sentiment.

Hank's purple body was starting to swell and grow. Now the two of them were heading for the window that led out to the balcony. There was a crash of glass and they passed out into the rainy night.

Their struggle continued out on the balcony; the wooden rail at the edge was the only thing keeping them from the long drop down to the pavement. It couldn't hold both their weight for very long.

"Daddy!" Hannah shrieked. *"Hank!!"*

There was a crunch, and the two plunged over the side of the mansion.

Two corpses laid out in the rain, the corpses of two men.

General Darwin's face was twisted up in a mask of rage. But Hank Howard, at last, had found peace.

11.

Funerals don't ever seem to happen on sunny days. It's funny because people die every day, and so funerals happen every day too. But it's always dark and cloudy when it's time to say the final goodbye to someone. Somehow every sunny day seems to have a cloudy one inside of it.

Hannah was one of the only people who had come to the service—Hank didn't have much family left, and so really it was just Sam who had showed up. Hannah was wearing a black mourning dress and a widow's veil. She and Hank hadn't had a chance to get married, but she still considered herself his wife in a way.

Sam was gone now, having gone back home, and she was alone with Hank's tombstone. She wanted to talk to him alone, and now she had her chance.

"Oh, Hank," she said quietly. She stared at the unmoving stone that bore his name. She sat for a while in silence, trying to move her lips but not finding the strength.

"I guess I'm not very good at talking to headstones," she said at last, awkwardly. "I—"

The tears came again.

"Oh God, Hank, I miss you. Do you know what I'd give just to see your face one more time? And to touch it...and kiss it...God. I'd give anything."

She wiped her face under her veil with a black-gloved hand.

"It's hard to forget what happened. I mean, you did kill my father. But I was blind—I didn't know he had a dark side. I didn't know how deep his evil ran. And you were just defending yourself. He tried to kill you...he would've, once you were no longer useful to him. It was his fault. All I—all I wanted for us to be together forever.

"But now everyone's gone. And I'm all alone."

She took out a single white rose from the folds of her dress, and placed it on the freshly-replaced soil.

"Goodbye, Hank. I love you."

She rose slowly, and then, with a final glance at the gravestone, stepped away. And she kept walking, without looking back, until she was gone.

Someone had been waiting for her to leave. Once he was sure that she was gone, Ray Garton staggered out from behind one of the tall monuments. He stepped drunkenly over to Hank's gravesite, a bottle of whiskey in his hand.

Garton's eyes read that name he hated so much: HENRY HOWARD. He clenched his fist and gnashed his teeth.

"I hope you're in Hell!" he cried. "Sitting on...Satan's...pitchfork!" Spittle flew free from his liquored-smelling mouth. "You unholy asshole," he added, muttering.

He tried to bore holes in the grave with his eyes; he was thinking of Lisa. He felt like crying.

But instead, a joke developed in mind—Garton always liked his jokes, even in the depths of grief. His bottle was empty now, down to the last drop, but he mimed pouring it over the grave.

"Wanna drink?" he slurred. Then he gave it a beat, pretending Hank had said something.

"Oh, wuzzat? Don't like liquor?"

Now, the punchline. He whipped out his *piece de la resistance* —his man-flesh.

"Well, have a drink a' this instead!"

And then he released a golden stream of that most indelicate of body fluids: piss.

Garton's face slumped into dumb satisfaction. Not only was he enjoying the grave-desecration, but it was a much-needed piss as well.

He was so satisfied that he was completely unprepared when two purple hands burst out of the grave.

Those hands curled into fists, and they *bonked* hard against the sides of Garton's head. The bald detective went cross-eyed and slumped to the ground.

TO BE CONTINUED…?!

The Bulk Who Walked the West

1912. The last days of the Old West.

The small town of Tumbleweed was cut off from the rest of the world. Located in the middle of one of the great American deserts, the minuscule burg was a reasonable enough place for a person to earn a living. Wasn't as dangerous as some towns still were, in spite of the isolation, unless one considered boredom a hazard. But there were card games in the saloon most days, and old Madame Modino ran a brothel in the upper part of the hotel. Liquor could be bought and there was some good eating at the local hash-house. And of course, there were cattle to be driven. Still good work for men who did that sort of thing out here. So as long as one had the will and the wit to make things work, life was a decent thing.

A large man was sitting at the local saloon, sipping his sarsaparilla. He was hunched over his glass like he was worried someone was gonna steal it. He wore a broad Mexican sombrero to shield himself from the sun.

The only other people in the bar besides him and the bartender was a group of four men who were playing poker. They were joking and chuckling amongst themselves, and seemed to be having a good time. If a person listened closely enough they could hear the coming and going of hands, without having to look over. And so it was plain to tell that a hand had just ended when a sudden silence overtook the quartet.

One of the men, speaking lowly, said something about cheating. It was just a mumbling of the word, but it hung in the air.

Tumbleweed was a quiet town but even in a quiet town, an accusation of cheating was no joke. Men got bullets in their hides for that.

"Cheatin'?" one of the men said. "You think I was *cheatin'*?"

"Now don't you get sore, Clem, I was jus'—"

"Stick 'em high, buckaroo!"

The man who the mumbler had called Clem had a six-gun in his hand. The accuser put his hands in the air, and started pleading for his life.

"Please, Clem, please, I beg ya, I weren't trying to say nothin' bad about yer, I was jus'—"

"You was just ruinin' my reputation in this town, is all!" Clem let out a cruel laugh. "You bet say yer prayers, y'old tenderfoot. I got ya dead to rights!"

Just then, the man at the bar sprung up and called out, "Stop right there!"

Now the man in the sombrero had a six-gun in *his* hand, trained right at Clem.

"Señor Gartón!" one of Clem's friends gasped. "H-hey, now, Clem didn't mean nothin' by what he said..."

"Like Hell!" Clem shouted. "You may be the Sheriff of this town, Ramon Gartón, but that don't mean a load a' bull to me. Now are you gonna do somethin' with that pea-shooter, or are ya gonna stand there and whistle—"

Gartón squeezed the trigger of his pistol, and blew Clem's piece straight out of his grip.

"He's like a devil!" one of the gamblers declared.

"He's the fastest shot in the West," said the man who'd first brought up cheating.

At once, all four men signed an agreement of peace that Sheriff Gartón drafted on the spot. He was as quick as a pen as he was his gun.

Gartón couldn't hold back the smile that was forming below his thick mustache. Nothing he liked better than settling disputes in his favorite saloon.

Outside that saloon, however, there was another threat to the peace of Tumbleweed. One that the streets of the town were too small to contain. It was only natural that trouble came spilling into the saloon, carried by the panicked form of Señorita Alvarez.

"*¡Señor Gartón! ¡Señor Gartón!*" she cried.

"*¿Selestina, que pasa?*"

"*¡Un hombre afuera! ¡Él tiene un gran agujero en él!*"

At once, the Sheriff bolted towards the street. He couldn't believe his ears.

Señorita Alvarez gathered her courage and ran out with him, to show him what she'd found. She took him down the dusty road to one of the snaking alleys that could be found next to Harry's Barbershop and Opium Den.

What the Sheriff saw in that alley made his heart skip a beat.

It was just as Selestina had said. There was a dead man with a big hole blown in him.

It looked like he'd been shot through with a cannon.

"*¿Qué le pasó?*"

The Sheriff couldn't answer her. He had no idea.

All he knew was, this was one of Skunk Blayden's men.

Skunk Blayden was one of the few people who could give Gartón indigestion. He was one of the new young punk crooks who were playing at being a 20th Century Jesse James. He and his men had been attacking homesteads outside of Tumbleweed for several weeks now, knocking people down and stealing their valuables.

And Gartón didn't have much in the way of help. Sure, he had some friends he could count on—his old pal Fuzzy Q. Jones would surely never turn down a call for deputization—but he needed an army to take down a monster like Blayden.

But who was it who had gunned down this hombre? Who was packing a gun that big?

Gartón knew he wouldn't sleep easy till he had figured it out.

* * *

Night fell, and Gartón was making the long walk back to his ranch. The moonlight left the mountains in the distance looking like waves of purple against the soft blackness. The sagebrush and the cacti stood still in the faint sunless chill, and the wind sang songs over the sandy expanse and the cracked red earth. Gartón whistled quietly to himself as he moseyed along.

Just then, something caught his eye. Something moving off in the distance.

Something charging towards him.

He stopped his march, and turned to stare off into the horizon. He tried to see what it was that was bearing down on him.

It had the running stride of a horse, but it couldn't be one. It was too big.

Yet at the same time, as it drew closer, he could see it had a man riding on it. It *was* a horse—a huge one, like something out of a myth.

And the rider was similarly huge. The size of him and his steed only got more and more apparent as they approached.

And horse and rider both—they were *purple*.

Gartón rubbed his eyes, but the sight didn't go away. There really was an enormous purple horse charging towards him, with an enormous purple man on its backside.

Gartón examined the man closely. Despite his size, he had found clothes that fit him. He was dressed in a black shirt that was covered by a red-brown rawhide jacket, whose sleeve tassels billowed behind him as he rode. He wore black chaps that were secured to his waist by a gigantic belt, upon which he wore a holster with a six-gun in it. Atop his head he'd donned a black Westerner's hat with a brown band.

He had to have been the owlhoot who had blown a hole in Blayden's man. That gun of his size was just the size for it.

Gartón was certain that the horse was going to run him over. But at the critical moment, when it was just a foot or two away from him, the titanic beast reared up before him, and left out a loud, rumbling neigh.

The rider stared at him, with wet, weary white eyes. Gartón was sure it was the face of the Devil.

Then the horse turned back around, and went back the way it came. Gartón stood frozen as the horse and rider galloped away into the distance, leaving a storm of dust behind them.

Gartón knew that that monster had to be an enforcer of Blayden's. Such a horrific beast could only be a servant of evil!

Gartón had a duty to perform. He would hunt down and destroy that demon, and his demon-stallion.

* * *

The next day, when Gartón was riding around town on patrol, he ran into a fellow horseman—Skunk Blayden.

With Blayden were two of his cronies, who Gartón dubbed Scar and Pimple, for the predominant features of their faces. They were as tough of customers as Blayden himself was. Blayden's face was very long and very sharp, and his silver hair looked it was made of blades. Speaking of blades, he had a proclivity towards licking them—at least, when he wasn't handling reins.

"Howdy, Sheriff—good to see ya."

Gartón tipped his hat and said, "Blayden."

"Do you know, Sheriff," Blayden said, "I think yer losin' your touch."

"You do, do you?" Gartón asked.

"One of my men was murdered last night, and it doesn't seem t'me like you've done anything about it."

Gartón felt the corner of his mouth rise. "Just 'cause I haven't made a public announcement doesn't mean I'm not going to do anything about it."

"Any clues on the case, Sheriff?"

"I've got my theories."

Yeah—like how Blayden had probably sicced the killer on the dead man for disobeying him. Blayden wasn't averse to getting rid of his own men when they inconvenienced him.

"Well, you keep on theorizing, Señor Gartón," Blayden laughed. "I'm sure it'll lead ya somewhere."

He and his two goons turned to ride off. Blayden shot a mocking glance over his shoulder as he departed.

"I hope it don't lead ya down a hole!" he added.

Gartón at least took a little solace in knowing that man was bound for Hell. He crossed himself whenever Blayden rode past; he had an evil stench about him. That was why men called him Skunk.

The day's sun was still shining down, though, and that meant that there were still a few good things ahead of Sheriff Gartón. Now he spotted one of those good things walking towards him.

The figure was unmistakable. That long blue dress, which trailed far behind its wearer, and the preposterous goggle-like glasses which sat based on that smooth nose—the only woman Gartón knew who wore such was one Madame Eliza van Tüttel.

"Ah, greetings, Señor Gartón," Madame Eliza said. "I don't suppose I could bother you into coming down off that horse for a chat?"

"For you, Eliza?" the Sheriff replied, cocking an eyebrow. "Anything."

He found a place to tie up his horse nearby, and he hopped off the saddle. She walked up to him, clutching her skirts with both hands. The two exchanged a significant look, and then, with a smile, Gartón gestured towards a nearby alleyway. The pair stepped into that alley together.

One of the merchants around here who sold goods on market day kept their stall stashed in this alley; they moved out it onto the street when it was time to sell. They kept a big black tarpaulin over it when it was not in use, and there were two stools inside, for the merchant and her young son. Gartón habitually used this stall to hold secret conversations.

"What's the matter, Eliza?" he asked, once they were situated. "Have you—have you seen something?"

The mysterious Dutchwoman was a superstitious type, and she believed in many uncanny things, none of which Gartón professed to understand. Madame van Tüttel was fond of telling people that she had the gift of second sight. And sometimes, Gartón almost believed her.

"I have had a strange vision of something out in the desert," she said. "Something I have never seen before."

"What was it?"

She frowned. "I had a dream. A strange dream."

He nodded. "Go on."

"I dreamt that the Earth was hollow, like an egg without a yolk. And inside of the Earth was where the waters of Time could be found."

Gartón followed along, but already he found her words confusing.

"I entered into the Earth, and I swam in the waters of Time," Eliza went on, "and in the heart of that great, churning ocean, there were places were Time froze and stood still, crystallizing into quartz rock.

"And in these crystals, all of Time could be seen. There was a light coming off of the stones that seemed to hamper my vision. But I saw glimpses of both the future and the past within those fractal surfaces."

"What sort of things did you see?" Gartón asked.

"What I saw in the crystals matters less than the fact that there is a place within the Earth where these crystals really exist."

Gartón winced. "Oh, Dios—listen, Eliza, I—"

"You don't believe me, I know," she interrupted. "But you have no other clues for finding out who *really* killed Blayden's man."

"...what?"

No one was supposed to know a man was killed last night. Blayden knew because the dead man worked for him, but there was no reason for Eliza to know a murder had been committed.

Unless *there* was some validity to her powers.

"I can show you the way with my dowsing-rod," the Dutch medium insisted.

"Look, Eliza, I do think you have some sort of ability," Gartón said, "but I'm not about to follow you out into the desert with you leading us around with a random stick."

"The stick that becomes a dowsing-rod is always carefully chosen. It's never random."

"Right..." Gartón rubbed the back of his neck. "I'm sorry, but I don't think I can take you up on it."

"You won't get another chance, Ramon." Those last two syllables surprised him—she'd never called him Ramon before.

"I'll talk to you tomorrow, Eliza," he said.

She didn't reply. She only stared at him. The stiffness of her lips implied she was harshly judging him.

But he wasn't one to believe in things like dowsing. Sticks off the ground didn't have the ability to lead people to hidden things.

And even if they could, there was clearly no such thing as "Time crystals." That was just spiritualist nonsense.

He walked away from his friend, and felt the compulsion suddenly to look back at her over his shoulder. He ignored it, feeling it was silly somehow.

* * *

Sheriff Gartón passed another difficult night. He had a nightmare in which Eliza was calling out to him through the darkness of the desert.

"Their greed is insatiable, Ramon...their thirst for riches cannot be quenched..."

Her face was strained and twisted, and her blue dress was billowing in what seemed to be a strong wind.

"There was one listening, Ramon...there was a man who knew of your secret place, who was listening to us..."

Gartón thrashed back and forth in the bed, a man tormented.

"They made me lead them, Ramon...they made me lead them out into the place where Time's hardened facets can be found..."

Gartón knew it was just a dream...it had to be. He wanted to wake up, even if he woke up screaming.

"It is too late, Ramon...too late...too late!"

The Sheriff shot up in bed, and his cry of terror surged out into the night.

Gartón didn't sleep for the rest of the night.

In the morning, Selestina Alvarez found Gartón and told him that Madame van Tüttel's house had been broken into and ransacked.

As for Madame van Tüttel herself, there was no sign of her.

Upon hearing the news, Gartón sat down on the ground for a long while, and thought about his friend.

* * *

He would've used the dowsing-rod to search for Eliza if it was still around. But they had made her take it with them—*they* being the Skunk Blayden gang. He was certain that it was Blayden who had taken her—there was no one else it could be.

He was similarly certain his dream was a message from Eliza. According to his dream, a member of the gang had overheard them talking about her vision. That man had passed on the story to Blayden, who thought that the crystals Eliza mentioned were some kind of treasure. The gang had then forced her out into the desert to show them the cave that she believed existed.

The night winds had swallowed the hoof-prints of their horses, so Gartón didn't even know which direction they'd gone in. It seemed hopeless.

But Eliza had seemed sure that these crystals could be found somewhere near to Tumbleweed. Gartón put faith in her words. He got up on his horse and got to searching. He started spiraling away from the town, looking on each pass for any sign of a cave.

For hours he rode. Over sandy plains and rocky hills he crossed; no canyon or mesa did he leave untouched. He rode and walked and climbed and ran until his boots were beaten white with dust, and his sombrero was ragged at the edges. The sun journeyed over his head, pulled by its invisible chariot, until the first traces of dusk were coming into the sky.

And no matter where he searched, all that time, he did not find a cave, nor any other sign of where Madame van Tüttel had been taken.

The final loop of his spiral ended with him over fifty miles away from the limits of Tumbleweed. Since it was getting dark, he figured it was time to go home—coyotes came out at night, and if a man wasn't careful a scorpion hidden in the darkness might sting and kill his horse. But disappointment left a bad taste in his mouth.

Just as he was finishing watering his horse, however, he heard the sound of thunder off in the distance. Like a brewing storm.

But he knew it wasn't thunder. He had heard the sound a couple nights before, when he saw that strange purple Bulk of a man riding his purple horse.

He scanned the horizon to see where it was coming from, and eventually he saw a silhouette against the twilight. The silhouette of a giant man riding an equally-huge horse. They were back again—and they were heading east.

Gartón was sure this strange man was an enforcer of Blayden's. And so now he, too, was heading east.

Gartón never wanted to let himself get too cocky—but here was an opportunity right at his feet. He was never one to pass up opportunity—not when a friend's life was on the line.

He chased the giant man across the desert, keeping at a distance so he wouldn't be spotted. The sky overhead grew darker and darker, but Gartón's eyes were keen even in darkness.

The chase went on for about twenty minutes, before eventually the Bulky rider started veering southward. Soon he had veered enough where he was heading due south; the Sheriff was right behind him. He figured they were making for a point somewhere west of the nearest town over, a border town called Santa Satanica.

Eventually, they came up on a rocky hill, and once they were at its foot, the violet titan slowed and dismounted his steed. He started walking quickly towards the closest ridge on the hill, marching with purpose in his steps. Though it was dark, Sheriff Gartón could see there was a cave mouth on that ridge.

Then there *was* something behind Eliza's vision. Maybe?

He left his own horse behind, and continued his pursuit of the Bulk (he had no other name for him). He stayed low to the ground, sneaking past the Bulk-horse where it remained standing. He was on the Bulk's tail as he climbed the hill and crossed into the cave. During the climb, Gartón observed that the giant man was looking around cautiously, as if this place was unfamiliar to him.

Maybe he wasn't a member of the Blayden gang after all.

Once he passed into the mouth of the cave, Gartón saw that the stone passage was lit by a shimmering blue light. He had never seen anything like it before. He didn't have long to study the light, however, as he could see that Bulk had already stopped walking not more than a few yards into the cave. He was kneeling down and examining something on the path.

He stood up, and Gartón saw he was cradling a limp body in his arms. A sad expression crossed his ugly, sagging face. It was the body of a woman he was holding—Eliza. And she was dead.

"Madre de Dios," Gartón exclaimed. "Eliza!"

The Bulk looked up at him in surprise, but Gartón didn't care about that monster now. He only cared about his friend.

He dashed over to the creature to examine her body—to his surprise, the giant man turned towards him to accommodate this. He gasped when he looked her over. They'd shot her in the back, the cowardly bastards!

"Oh, Eliza...they shouldn't have done this to you."

He could see now how delicately the Bulk was holding the body. With one huge, purple hand, the Bulk reached up and took his hat off his head in a gesture of respect.

"I can see now I misjudged you," Gartón said. "I feared you, and the power you clearly represent. But I can see now you are no servant of the Devil, nor of Skunk Blayden."

The Bulk shook his head no.

"You're here...to hunt down Blayden, aren't you?"

The Bulk nodded yes to that.

"Well, he's here. Don't need a dowsing-rod to know that now," Gartón said. "I don't know why you're going after Blayden, and I don't care. All I need to know is: are you with me?"

The Bulk nodded again, and then let out a raging cry of vengeance. Gartón couldn't help but shout with him.

And then, without further ado, the two of them took off charging into the cavern, in search of their enemy.

Their charge was not a long one. The tunnel they'd entered into was short, and it quickly opened up into an enormous chamber—one which seemed to take up half the hill they were standing inside.

Suspended from the ceiling like a stalactite was the source of the unearthly blue light. It was an enormous quartz-like crystal. It shimmered with a beauty neither Gartón nor the Bulk had seen before.

How no one had found this crystal before, they had no idea— they didn't know how long it had been slumbering here, waiting to be discovered. Or maybe, it had been found many times, by many people, and changed hundreds of lives over thousands of years—always in secret.

The two stared in the crystal, unable to help themselves. At once, before their minds could be steeled against the intensity of such a thing, a number of images flashed in front of them. The past, the future, they all spilled wide open, as they did commonly to Eliza in her visions.

At once, Gartón understood something of the nature of the creature that stood beside him. To him, the Bulk had appeared out of nowhere, a seeming freak of nature. But there had been others, all through human history, appearing exactly where they were needed to be. Past eras that Gartón's brain strained to comprehend were full of these Bulks. Ordinary people were mutated into them by strange forces beyond their imagination, and they became avengers of the innocent—time and time again.

Whenever one died of old age or misadventure or conspiracy by their enemies, then another would immediately be shifted to take their place.

They were still freaks of nature, these Bulk creatures, but they were bound into humanity's very lifeblood somehow. They were a cosmic necessity.

Gartón could only watch enraptured as the cycle continued into times he would never live to see. The crystal imbued on him some knowledge of the names and attributes of these various Bulks...

He saw the Pulp Bulk of the 1930s, a genius gadgeteer whose purple widow's peak hair glistened like metal...

He glimpsed the Acid Bulk of the 1960s, whose purple hide was flecked with other colors, like the splatter of a tie-dye shirt...

He spotted the Amazing Bulk of the 2010s, who fought for love against a mad scientist and a tall, muscular woman whose name meant death...

And then, beyond: the Cyborg Bulk of the Year 2300, who had computers grafted into his brain and muscles. The Space Bulk of

2666, who was so strong he could jump from planet to planet. The Solar Bulk of 3450, who could use suns as gateways to travel the universe. And in a year so far beyond that it had no number—Earth and all of its colony worlds were the homes of a species of Bulks—the Final Stage in the long game called Terrestrial Evolution...

Yes, in the future, the far distant future, all the descendants of all the people who were alive today in 1912 would be purple, gyrating, hairless, half-amorphous muscle-beasts possessed of enormous physical powers...

Gartón could scarcely believe how wondrous and horrible it seemed all at once.

The Bulk, if he could speak in this form, would also remark on how strange and beautiful Time now seemed to him.

For a long time it seemed like nothing could ever pull their eyes away from the visions playing out in the giant crystal. But then, both men heard a thin chuckle split the air. It was such an evil-sounding chuckle that they had to look down at its source.

Skunk Blayden was approaching them from the far end of the cavern, licking the blade of his knife as he often did.

"So, you found me at last, Señor Gartón," he snickered, between licks. "I'm afraid it's too late to stop me now. I've found this treasure. Me an' the boys thought the physical crystal itself would make us rich, but the future it's shown me is valuable beyond any price."

"What are you talking about, Blayden?" Gartón asked. "What future do you mean?"

"The future isn't just one thing, Sheriff," Blayden said. "It's a whole tree—every moment in Time is a tree. Every moment has the potential to branch off into a million different futures. An' in the timeline where I *seize* the power of this crystal, and make it a part of myself, I establish a criminal dynasty that rules the world fer seven hundred years." He waved his knife at them arrogantly. "That's the sorta future *I* like!"

"You intend to steal the power of this crystal somehow, and..."

"An' become a god, Sheriff Gartón. An immortal, undyin' god."

"You're insane."

"All great men are considered insane at first, Sheriff! But I'm different. You and yer big purple friend can't do nothin' to stop us." He snapped his fingers, and suddenly an army of men spilled out of the cave. There were dozens of them, all armed to the teeth.

But Gartón wasn't scared.

"I wouldn't underestimate this big hombre," Gartón said. "He already made one of your men into Swiss cheese, Blayden. I wouldn't cross him."

"It's too late, Sheriff! I'm already connected to the power of the crystal. Look! It's wanin'. 'Cause its power is goin' into *me*."

It was true—the giant quartz was slowly losing its glow. Gartón didn't know how Blayden was doing it, but that didn't matter now. He had to stop this from happening, even if he barely understood was "this" was.

He drew his pistol, and Blayden's face lit up, like Christmas had come early for him. The Bulk saw Gartón's draw and pulled out his own colossal gun.

"Well, that's just what I like," Blayden said. "Always wanted to rub ya out, Sheriff! And now it seems I'll get my wish!" He glanced back at his boys, and raised his hands towards the dimming crystal. "Get 'im, you owlhoots!"

The army of men charged towards them, guns blazing.

Gartón had to get to cover. Fortunately he was near a large stalagmite, and it proved adequate shielding against the spray of incoming gunfire. The Bulk held his ground, and to Gartón's amazement, most of the bullets bounced off the titan's purple skin. Some managed to pierce it, but the giant gunslinger hardly seemed to notice the spurts of purple blood that erupted from these wounds.

Instead, the big man just aimed his hand-cannon at the charging crowd, and let them have it.

The shell-like bullets ripped through the men like flame through silk. At least three dropped every time he squeezed the trigger; and his third shot nabbed seven. It was a total bloodbath, and at first it seemed he was totally invincible—this was gonna be a cakewalk. But even a Bulk could only be stung so many times.

Gartón stayed tucked behind cover, letting the giant do most of the work. But the Bulk only had a six-shooter, and so he had to stop to reload once his sixth bullet was gone. And as he did so, Blayden's men spilled onto him like Lilliputians onto Gulliver, stabbing him with their knives and bayonets. The giant let out a roar of pain and flailed his arms wildly, trying to shake the attackers off.

Here was where the Sheriff came in. He zeroed his pistol in on the stabbers, and blasted them off of the Bulk's backside. The Bulk rallied when he saw Gartón come to his defense, and he used his fists against the goons unfortunate enough to be directly in front of him. He flung them across the cavern, bags of broken bones.

Eventually, Gartón ran out of bullets, just as the big brawler had. He didn't carry a knife, but he had a lasso, and he had a good aim with it. As men continued to swarm onto the Bulk, he threw the rope at them from behind the rocks, and jerked them down onto the ground. He tugged them with such force that they went flying off their feet and smacked their heads on the hard cave floor. They went to sleep when that happened. Then Gartón worked the lasso off of them and tossed it again at a fresh victim.

One of the thugs remembered that his boss wanted Gartón dead too, and he broke away from the crowd charging the Bulk to take on the Sheriff. Gartón couldn't rope the man before he was upon him, and so he had to take to his fists. The two scuffled brutally on the stony ground, swapping fierce kicks and punches —Gartón fought like a wildcat, for his life was on the line.

The Bulk saw his new friend was in trouble, but he couldn't do anything to help. His own fists were needed to knock away the last survivors of the gang, who were fighting now to avenge their fallen brothers. His arms whipped out left and right, and one by one the gang thinned to nothing.

Gartón was pinned down by his attacker, but he had one last tactic, something that always worked. His knee came up and hit the man right in the cojones. The hired gun groaned stiffly and slumped off of the Sheriff. Gartón stood up just as the Bulk went charging at Blayden.

But Blayden had already taken much of the strange energies hidden in that crystal; and now, he could use some of that power to defend himself. When the Bulk's colossal punches thrust his way, a crackling bluish light appeared that blocked the blows with an impenetrable force. The Bulk roared and did his best to break through, but it was no use. The sparking force kept him back from his enemy.

Blayden laughed triumphantly: "I am almost there!" he declared. "Soon, the Blayden dynasty will become eternal! My son, and his son after him, and his son after all of us, will rule the world. The name of Blayden will eclipse those of Napoleon, of Alexander, of Caesar! And we shall make new laws for all mankind! Laws that honor the universal truth: *Blayden is supreme!*"

The Bulk stopped his assault—he saw it was no use. He looked back at Gartón, hoping he had an answer. But this was all beyond the humble Sheriff's powers of discernment.

The Bulk craned his head up to the crystal, and Gartón followed his gaze. A ripple of futures appeared before them once again. But the images could barely be seen in the darkened facets.

Gartón felt like it wasn't fair—something this beautiful shouldn't be transformed into a tool of evil. He'd rather it was destroyed than twisted in that way. But even destroying it felt like some degree of blasphemy.

Still, he knew already that he and Bulk were thinking the same thing.

This power could not belong to Skunk Blayden. No matter the cost.

In fact, the Bulk had realized this before Gartón had. And so he was already loading an enormous bullet into his revolver.

Gartón realized what the giant man was about to do. He started breathing heavily. "How—how do you know that's safe?" he asked.

The Bulk looked at him, but made no sign of having heard him. He was grimly determined to accomplish the task he'd chosen.

"If we destroy it—and that power is unleashed—it could engulf us," Gartón speculated.

This time the Bulk nodded. But his drive didn't fade.

Instead, he looked at Gartón and pointed to the cave exit.

"I—I can't let you sacrifice your life," Gartón sputtered.

But the Bulk's face said it all: *my life was over the moment I received this curse.*

At least, that was what Gartón thought he was thinking. He had no way to be sure.

He hesitated only a moment longer. Then, he started running for the exit, Blayden's mocking laugh echoing behind him.

"Fleein' like a yella coward, are ya, Sheriff? Why miss all the fun?" And the light flashed around his body, glowing so bright that it illuminated the bones of his skeleton. "Ya don't wanna miss my *apotheosis*, do ya?"

Gartón could barely look at Blayden. He was changing— gaining height and depth—and other dimensions too. Dimensions which Gartón couldn't fully comprehend.

He placed his hands over his face, and he ran until he could feel the moonlight on him.

Behind him, the Bulk took aim the hardened fragment of Time...

...and he squeezed the trigger.

There was a terrific blast from the cave, following swiftly by the rumbling of stone. Gartón pulled his hands away from his face and looked back, only to see that the cave was crumbling in on itself.

He ran forward a moment, his instincts thinking maybe he stood a chance of running in and saving the Bulk before it was too late.

But it was already too late. Anything inside of that cave would now be buried under hundreds of tons of rock.

Gartón's arms slumped by his sides. He'd won—but the price had been high.

Suddenly, however, he had the feeling of eyes on him—like he wasn't alone.

He whirled around, and saw the figure of Madame van Tüttel standing before him.

"Eliza?!" he cried. "You're alive! How—"

She stopped him with a raised hand. "I'm not alive, Ramon. I am well and truly dead."

"Then—"

"I am on my way to a better place—but I have stopped along my way to thank you for putting right the circumstances of my death."

"I—" He couldn't believe she was standing there—she looked so real. "I am...honored to have helped you, one last time."

"I'm afraid you and I are bound to a sad cycle, Ramon Gartón. It seems that throughout all our lives, throughout all of Time, you are doomed to witness me die in front of you, time and time again. Through blood and metempsychosis alike, our tragedy worms a dark path through the ages..."

"If souls do come back, I promise I will save yours," he said.

She smiled. "There is so little we can do to defy Fate. Why change what is set in stone?" He opened his mouth to protest, but she went on: "I must go now, Ramon. The forces that guide us won't let me tarry forever. Goodbye."

"Eliza, wait—!"

He reached a hand out towards her, but in the blink of an eye, she vanished, as if she was never there.

Gartón took a moment to close his eyes and honor the memory of his friend.

Then he heard his horse call to him. It had stayed loyally where he had left it; the Bulk's horse, perhaps sensing the loss of its master, had run off somewhere, and could not be found. Gartón rejoined his steed and began his long journey back to Tumbleweed.

He looked back at the collapsed cave, where the Bulk was buried. The hill itself was his funeral cairn—only appropriate for a giant like him.

Gartón clicked his tongue and shook his head. "Who was that purple man?"

About the Author

Atom Mudman Bezecny is a prolific American author, editor, and publisher whose work spans science fiction, fantasy, horror, and surrealist pulp. With a deep love for genre storytelling and outsider art, she has authored dozens of novels and novellas — many of which explore identity, transformation, and the boundaries of reality through a distinctly queer and experimental lens.

As the founder of Odd Tales Productions and PhantomEye Press, Atom champions bold, unconventional voices in modern pulp and underground literature. Her writing often pays homage to the aesthetics of vintage genre fiction while subverting its norms with wit, weirdness, and emotional depth. Known for her prolific output and fearless imagination, she has become a defining figure in the world of contemporary speculative fiction.

Atom infuses her stories with personal insight, symbolic resonance, and a deep commitment to creative freedom. Whether reworking pulp archetypes or building strange new worlds, her work is always vivid, unapologetic, and unmistakably her own.

Also by Atom Mudman Bezecny

So Be It...Desecrator

Vengeance

The Bryan Gospels

The Synchronicity Wizards

Tomb of the Ancient Ones

Nick Tredor Adventures

The Mushroom

Kingdom Cryptiqqa

Night of the Living Dead: Beast Wars

Patrona